MW01141334

Make Me a Memory

Make Me a Memory

by Tamra Norton

Bonneville Books
Springville, Utah

ISBN: 1-55517-866-9
v. 2

Published by Bonneville Books,
an imprint of Cedar Fort, Inc.
925 N. Main Springville, Utah, 84663
www.cedarfort.com

Distributed by:

Cover design by Nicole Williams
Cover design © 2005 by Lyle Mortimer

Printed in the United States of America
10 9 8 7 6 5 4 3 2

Printed on acid-free paper.

Dedication

To my sweet Allison Lynne. And to the children of our dedicated men and women serving abroad in the U.S. military. They honor our nation by their dedicated sacrifice, you honor them by making memories while apart, and I attempt to honor you all with this story.

Acknowledgments

I would like to thank my publisher, Cedar Fort, Inc., for bringing this timely story to the many children and families who I hope will find comfort and even a few laughs within its pages.

I owe a great debt of appreciation to the Houston Society of Children's Book Writers and Illustrators and in particular to Kathi Appelt and the Joan Lowery Nixon Award for recognizing something of promise in the first chapter of this story. Thank you for sharing your wisdom and guidance throughout this endeavor. You are a treasured mentor, as well as friend.

I am grateful to my dear friend Josi Kilpack and to my critique buddies—Deborah Frontiera, Millie Martin, and Hanako Brown—for their valued input. I would also like to thank the LDStorymakers for challenging me on a daily basis to become a better writer.

Finally, a big thank-you goes to my wonderful family for embracing my creative side, even if it means eating frozen pizza and corn dogs on a regular basis. I love you very much!

1

The Move

It's not a very smart thing to spit out the window of a moving car. Of course, I learned this the hard way. When I took the mouthful of orange juice, I was only thinking about how thirsty I was. And tired. I'd been sitting in a hot car all day long with that bottle of juice.

It's funny because apple juice tastes pretty good hot. And so does lemon juice—if you add a little honey. But drinking hot orange juice is about as much fun as drinking the last of the milk in your cereal bowl. Especially after it's been sitting for an hour and a few mushy pieces are still floating around the top and your mom can't seem to quit going on and on about the starving children in Africa and the shame of wasting good food.

I tried about as hard as any eleven-and-a-half-year-old could to spit the hot, sour orange juice out of the window of The Bruise—that's what Mom calls our old minivan, I think because it's kind of purplish-reddish, like the color of a bruise—but the juice splashed back into my face and hair and on Dad's black baseball cap that I was wearing. Somehow it even managed to spray Mom.

"Allison Jayne Claybrook, quit goofing around and get your head back in this car. Do you want me to get in a wreck?"

Just as I sat my rear end back on the seat, Spencer, my five-year-old brother, must have woken up—probably from Mom's hollering. She seemed to be hollering more than usual lately— hollering and crying.

Spencer, who has Dad's blond hair but brown eyes like me and Mom, was stretching his arms and trying to speak at the same time his mouth was gaped open in a huge yawn. Most people might not have understood what he said, but I did.

"Mommy, are we almost there yet?"

Now I'm usually a patient person, but my little brother had asked this same question in one form or another at least eight bazillion times a day since we left our home at Fort Hood and pulled out of Killeen, Texas, two days earlier. School had just let out for summer vacation, only we weren't going on vacation. We were leaving for good.

I turned around from my spot in the front seat of The Bruise and gave Spencer *the look:* eyebrows furrowed, nose scrunched a little, lips pinched together. I guess I didn't scare him into hushing up because the little dweeb just pointed his stubby finger at my wet, stinky-sticky face and laughed.

Mom didn't seem to notice.

"Yes, Buddy, we're almost there."

Dad had always been the one who called Spencer "Buddy," so I thought it was a little strange that Mom would start now. Maybe she was just trying to help Spencer remember Dad. After all, it could be a whole year before we see him again. That's twelve months . . . fifty-two weeks . . . three hundred and sixty-five days . . . winter, spring, summer, and fall.

"Why did Dad have to go to Iraq anyway?" I asked as I took Dad's baseball cap off and began wiping the juice from my face and hair with the front of my T-shirt. It already had tan root beer stains on it from lunchtime when my disgusting little brother made me choke while I was sipping my soda. He'd stuck two French fries up his nose and said he was an elephant and the fries were his tusks. The kid loved animals.

Mom handed me a few tissues. "Honey, Dad had to go to Iraq. He's doing his job as a soldier. This is what the engineering corps does. They help rebuild roads, bridges, and other things damaged in the war."

"But why did *we* have to leave Killeen? All my friends are in Texas. And I don't know anyone who lives with both their grandma *and* great-grandma. Well ... except Tiffany Sherwood, and that's because her mom and dad got a divorce." I quit talking for a second because a horrible thought invaded my brain. *What if everyone in Edna, Idaho, thought my mom and dad were divorced? Great!* "And what a crazy name—*Edna*, Idaho. What am I supposed to do in a place called Edna, Idaho? I bet there's only old people there."

Mom looked at the road and shook her head ever so slightly as she spoke. "Allison, Allison, Allison. *Where* do you get these ideas? And there's plenty of stuff to do in Edna. Remember . . . *I* grew up there. My friend Trudy has a daughter near your age. We'll get you two together. You can hang out."

I wasn't convinced that I'd like living in Edna,

but Mom sure was doing her best to make me feel good about this move. "And Grandma is full of all sorts of fun. I bet she'll teach you how to bake bread."

"Oh, boy." I didn't even try to sound excited.

"Maybe we can even find someone to teach you how to ride a horse."

Now *that* sounded exciting—but I didn't want Mom to know. I was still mad at her about the move.

After a few moments, I looked over at Mom. She'd been driving The Bruise for three straight days and she looked really tired—more tired than usual. Mom let out a long, deep sigh as she briefly glanced at my sticky face before turning her eyes back to the road.

"I wasn't going to tell you this yet—I *shouldn't* tell you this yet." Mom took another deep breath, letting the air slowly pass through her lips. "But I can see, Miss Allie, that you're not going to give me any peace unless you know the whole truth." I had no idea what Mom was talking about, but a slight uneasy feeling settled deep inside my stomach, kind of like when the teacher tells you to put away your books 'cause it's time for a big test.

I looked over at Mom, and she had her hand on her belly—she must have had that same uneasy feeling in her stomach too.

Mom waited a while before saying anything. And just when I began to wonder if maybe she was so tired from driving for three straight days that she'd forgotten she was about to tell me the "whole truth," she turned to me briefly. Her eyes looked a little excited but also afraid. "I'm pregnant, Allie. We're going to have a baby."

"Really?" I immediately forgot about Edna and horses and not having friends. We were going to have a new baby. Maybe it would be a girl—a sister. I'd given up on that idea over four years ago when Spencer was born. Mom called him her "miracle baby." She didn't think she'd ever be able to have more children—and with Spencer as a little brother, sometimes I wished she hadn't.

I looked back at Spencer to see his reaction, but he was busy licking his finger and drawing a picture on the window with his spit.

"We found out just a month before Daddy was scheduled to leave." Mom was patting her belly even though it wasn't even poking out yet, and she almost looked like she wanted to smile.

I was surprised about having a new baby. I'd have to get used to the idea. I'm pretty good at getting used to new things. When I was little, I got used to eating green beans when Mom told me I couldn't have any dessert until I ate my vegetables. We were having Mom's chewy, homemade chocolate chip cookies that night, and, well, I'd probably eat a worm just to have my mom's cookies. I still don't like green beans, but I hold my breath and eat them anyway if dessert is good enough.

And this past year I got used to saying "yes, ma'am" or "no, ma'am" to Mrs. Halberg, my fifth-grade teacher. She was old enough to be a grandma, and if you didn't say "ma'am" after answering "yes" or "no," she'd say "Excuse me? Excuse me?" over and over until you said it right. Even though I was certain I'd get used to the idea of having a new baby around, I still wished we hadn't left Texas.

"You're being awful quiet, Allie. What are you thinking?"

"Dad's not even going to be here when our baby's born, is he? Isn't it important to him? Why is being a soldier more important to Dad than our baby?"

Next thing I knew, Mom had pulled The Bruise over to the side of the freeway and stopped. Then she turned her entire body so it was facing me and reached over to take my hand—it was still a little sticky from the whole orange juice thing, but Mom didn't seem to mind.

"Allison, your Daddy loves us all very much, *even* this little baby growing inside of me. But he has a very important duty to keep." Mom let go of my hand and reached up to brush the front of my hair with her fingers. She didn't seem to mind the wet sticky mess up there either.

"Now, honey, it's a lot of hard work to have a baby without Daddy here. I'm going to need you and Spencer to be real understanding and helpful until he gets back. Can you do that for me? Can you help me out until Daddy comes home? It'll mean a lot to me if I know I can count on you."

Mom was suddenly quiet for a minute, and when she finally spoke it was almost a whisper. "You know, Allie . . . he'd be here if there was any way he could."

Mom's wasn't crying, but I could tell that she was having a fight with her eyes to keep those tears from spilling out. It scared me a little to see Mom so upset and I wasn't quite sure what to do, so after a moment I tried to reach over to give her a hug, but my seat belt pressed me back down into my seat. I quickly reached down, released the strap and leaned over into Mom's arms, smashing Dad's black baseball cap right between us. Now I could really tell she was crying because her body was shaking.

As the two of us hugged and cried, I remembered the words Dad had said to me the night before he left for Iraq. Now I understood.

"Allie . . . Mom's really going to need your help while I'm away." That was all he said. Dad just quit talking and hugged me tight for a long time. Then he placed his favorite black baseball cap on my head and whispered in my ear, "I love you, Cracker Jack. Don't ever forget that." Dad always called me Cracker Jack because he said I was full of surprises.

Now, I pulled back from Mom, poked at Dad's baseball cap with my fist to unsmoosh it, and placed it back onto my head.

"I promise, Mom. I promise to help." And I meant it too. This new baby was important to Mom—and Dad. But even knowing all that, it still didn't seem right—or fair—that he couldn't be with us.

Mom reached out to wipe the tears from my cheek as we sat in The Bruise on the side of the highway until that familiar voice broke into the silence.

"Mommy, are we almost there yet?"

2

Nanna and Me

"Well, just look at this girl!" Grandma, who was shorter than Mom and a little bit chubby, was almost squishing my cheeks in the palm of her hands as she examined my face after I got out of The Bruise. "Lauren, she looks just like you did at this age."

For as long as I can remember, people have told me that I look like my mom—I liked this because

Mom is one of the prettiest women I know (except for maybe when she's been driving The Bruise for three straight days). We both have dark brown hair and eyes that match. And if Grandma thought we looked alike, then it must be true.

Mom reached over and removed Dad's baseball cap from my head. My hands went up to stop her, but she was too quick. Then she picked up a clump of my brown hair that was stuck together with dried orange juice and let it fall. "You should see Miss Allie here when she's not wearing orange juice and root beer. She actually cleans up pretty good—and Spencer too."

"Where *is* my Spencer?" Grandma asked.

But my little brother was nowhere in sight. The minute we pulled up in front of Grandma's big yellow house, he got out and started running around to the backyard. Every day while we were driving, Mom had told him all about the big yellow house that our great-great-grandpa built a hundred years ago. Outside there was a tire swing in the huge cottonwood tree, a strawberry patch, a chicken coop, and beautiful lilac bushes. Since Spencer wasn't even born the last time we were there, he didn't know about all the cool stuff at Grandma's house. I guess I'd forgotten most of it too, but I tried not to look too excited. After all, I was still mad about this move.

"Spencer," Mom hollered.

I pointed to the side of the house that I'd watched my little brother vanish behind. "I think he went that way."

Grandma reached for my hand like I was still a little kid. "Let's go see where that grandson of mine has run off to. And I'll introduce you to Abe—he's been keepin' up the lawn for me since Grandpa passed away." Our grandpa had died several years earlier. To be honest, I could hardly remember him.

Just as we were rounding the corner of Grandma's big yellow house, we heard several squawks and a really loud squeal. There was no mistaking that last noise. I'd heard it probably every day for the past five years. Most recently, I'd heard it when Spencer caught one of those green anole lizards in our backyard in Killeen. He was so proud of that creepy thing, waving it around and showing it off. Well, that green anole must've gotten real mad 'cause he bit down on Spencer's finger and wouldn't let go for a million bucks. Boy, could my little brother ever squeal—and now he was at it again somewhere behind Grandma's house. I wondered what had got him this time.

"Abraham Lincoln!" Grandma was shouting at the scruffy little brown goat with a black beard that was chasing my little brother around the big backyard. It reminded me of how Mom would call me by my full name, Allison Jayne Claybrook, when she really wanted to get my attention.

While Grandma kept hollering, Mom ran out to Spencer and scooped him up into her arms. Spencer was carrying a brown egg in each hand, and his face looked as scared as a turkey on Thanksgiving. I also noticed that the door to the chicken coop was wide open and a dozen or so chickens had scattered throughout Grandma's back lawn.

Grandma walked up next to Mom and Spencer, shaking her finger at the goat with the black beard. "You leave my grandson alone, you silly goat."

I thought it was funny that Grandma was talking to a goat like it could understand her. Maybe it did because the goat with the black beard lowered its brown head like it was sad or something and walked out toward the middle of the lawn where it started nibbling on a patch of tall grass. Now I knew what Grandma meant by Abe "keeping up the lawn."

"Lauren, put that boy down," Grandma said, this time waving her finger at Mom. Now I remembered just how good Grandma was at giving orders. "You shouldn't be lifting anything heavy."

"I realize that, Mother, but what am I supposed to do when your crazy goat is chasing after my son? And, what did you call him—Abe?" Mom put

Spencer down, took the brown eggs from him, but kept a firm hold on his hand.

"I think Abe was just protecting the chicken coop from this strange boy." Grandma ruffled her fingers through Spencer's blond hair, and I could tell by the way he scrunched up his nose and tilted his head that he didn't like it.

"Grandma," I asked. "Why did you call that goat Abraham Lincoln?"

"Well, Allie, I think ol' Abe kind of resembles our sixteenth president of the United States with his black beard and long, slender face. Don't you?"

To be honest, I thought Grandma had quite an imagination. He didn't look a bit like Abraham Lincoln. He just looked like a scruffy old goat. Grandma must be getting pretty old like everyone else in this town. When goats start looking like people, it's time to move away from Edna, Idaho.

"Sure." I said unconvinced, and looked up at Mom, who looked like she wanted to laugh.

"I think you need new glasses, Mother," said Mom.

"I have to use the bathroom!" Spencer suddenly wailed while tugging on Mom's arm.

At that moment, I noticed the little dweeb had taken the baseball cap from Mom, and now it was covering his messy blond hair. I reached over and quickly plucked it from his head.

"That's *my* hat," I said a little louder than I should have as I pulled it back onto my head, securing it snugly. I knew Dad didn't want me screaming at my little brother, but sometimes I just can't help it.

Spencer started to protest, but his whine was cut short by Grandma's voice. "Come on, Spencer, the bathroom's this way."

The little guy seemed to forget about the baseball cap as we all headed to the side door that led into the kitchen of the big yellow house.

"Is Nanna still up?" Mom asked Grandma. Nanna was Grandma's mom—my great-grandma— but we've always called her Nanna. I'm not sure why. To me it sounded like we were calling her a banana. Now that just didn't seem right. I think we should call the goat Nanna, and Great-Grandma something cool like Granny or GG.

"Yep, she's in the living room." Grandma opened the screen door to the kitchen and we all walked in. "But she probably won't remember you. Nanna even forgets who I am much of the time."

When Grandma started talking about Nanna's memory, I remembered back in Killeen when we were eating dessert (I'd eaten my vegetables that night). Mom told us that there are times when Nanna forgets she's just eaten a dish of ice cream or taken her pills. Mom said Grandma has to keep track of stuff like this or it could be dangerous. That night I tried to pretend that I'd forgotten to eat my dessert so I could get seconds. Mom didn't think it was funny, but Dad laughed until Mom scrunched up her face at him.

"The strange thing about Alzheimer's," said Grandma, "is that it usually takes the short term memory first. Nanna can remember almost every detail of her childhood here in Edna and growing up in this house, but she can't remember what day it is."

"Is all of this normal?" Mom asked.

"It can be," Grandma replied.

"I have to go *now*, Mommy!" Spencer squealed.

"All right, all right—I'll show you where the bathroom is."

Spencer and Mom took off down the hall, and Grandma reached out for my hand. "Allison, do you want to go say hello to Nanna?"

"I guess," I said, but I really wasn't sure I wanted to say hello to someone who sometimes forgot who her own daughter was and couldn't even remember if she ate a dish of ice cream. I mean, really now. It was just so hard to imagine someone would forget about eating *ice cream!*

I also wondered what it would be like living in a house with someone so old. Would I have to be quiet all the time? That would never work for Spencer, who liked to howl at the moon at night and pretend he was a rooster in the morning. Remember, the kid liked animals—except for goats, I guess.

And would I be able to have friends over? Would I even make any new friends here in this tiny little hick town? I wanted to go back to Killeen—back to our little house on base—back to when Dad was home.

Grandma led me into the living room where Nanna was sitting. I think I was about five years old the last time I was at Grandma's house. Everything looked familiar—even Nanna with her white hair. She was wearing a white sweater over a pink and blue housedress and was sitting in a pink recliner near a window covered with billowy white curtains. She seemed to match the room—like she belonged there.

Nanna looked over at me and then turned to Grandma with a puzzled expression.

"Nanna, this is Allison—Lauren's daughter. Remember, I told you that they would be staying with us while Allison's daddy is away.

The old woman gave me a warm smile and when she talked it was as if she was talking to a baby, not an eleven-and-a-half-year-old. "Well, hello there." I looked over at Grandma but she just smiled at me too.

"Hi," I replied. As I looked at Nanna, I couldn't help but notice her skin—it was almost see-through. On her hands she had a lot of brown spots and purple veins that seemed to poke out. Her hair was kind of fluffy, almost like cotton, and I don't think there was a single part of her face that didn't have a wrinkle on it.

"I'll let you two visit for a bit while I go check on dinner." Grandma said as she turned to leave the living room. "We'll be sittin' down to a nice meal before too long."

I wanted to tell Grandma to stay; to reach out and pull back on her two long apron strings hanging down her back, like I was slowing down a team of horses. But before the words could form in my mouth and my hands could reach out to grab those apron strings, Grandma was gone.

Nanna looked at me from across the room with the evening sun filtering through the curtains, and for a moment it looked like she recognized me—I wasn't sure. I was six and a half years older now than the last time I saw her, so I looked much more grown up. At least *I* thought so. But as I walked closer to her chair, I noticed that her eyes looked cloudy, like looking through dirty bath water.

Now, I realized that Nanna had definitely changed. She was also six and a half years older and had some Old-Timer's disease that was taking away her memory. It made me wonder if I'd start forgetting things when I got older. After all, Mom could *never* remember where she put her sunglasses and keys. And sometimes Dad would call me Spencer, or call my little brother Allie. Even Mom does it now and then. How could someone forget their own kid's name?

"Excuse me." Nanna's words broke into my thoughts. "But do you know when Daddy will be back?"

I was a little puzzled. Was Nanna asking about *my* dad? Maybe her memory wasn't all that bad.

I relaxed a little. "Dad won't be back for maybe a long time."

Nanna let out a weary sigh. "I really miss him, don't you?" She turned and looked out the window, and I got the feeling that maybe she didn't know I was there anymore. She must have been thinking about Dad.

Next thing I knew, I was thinking about him too—how he liked to play tickle monster with Spencer and me. How he would wake us up early on Saturday mornings so we could watch Bugs Bunny and Road Runner together while we ate our sugary cereal in the living room, sitting on the floor. Mom never found out—or at least she never said anything.

Nanna probably didn't know my dad all that

well, but finding out that someone else missed him like I did made me feel better—and miss him even more. I decided Nanna wasn't all that scary. Not like I thought at first. In fact, maybe she was the only one that understood how I felt.

"Yeah," I finally replied. "I really do miss Dad."

● ● ● ● ●

Dear Dad,

I know it will take a long time before you actually get this letter. I looked on a map and Iraq and Idaho are super far apart. Grandma said that she'd show me how her computer works tomorrow so I can send you an e-mail. It will be a lot quicker. But I thought I'd write this letter anyway to tell you that we made it to Edna, Idaho. I can tell you right now that it's going to take me a long time to get used to this place. Mom keeps telling me that I will. Oh, and Nanna misses you too, Dad, and Grandma has a crazy goat that she thinks looks like Abraham Lincoln—weird—and the best part is that I'm going to learn how to ride horses.

Love, Allie

P.S. Thanks for the baseball cap. When I wear it, I think of you.

P.P.S. Mom told me about the baby. That's pretty cool. It better be a girl, though!

3

Nighttime Noises

I didn't sleep well my first night in the big yellow house in Edna, Idaho—*couldn't* sleep. My first problem was that I had slept a good chunk of the day in the front seat of The Bruise, so I really wasn't all that tired.

My next problem was that I had to share a room with Spencer. I knew Spencer liked to imitate animals during the day, but since we've never had to share a room, I didn't know that he continued into the wee hours of the night. By the noise coming out of his five-year-old face, I would have sworn I was sharing my room with a great big momma pig. Actually, I think it's called a sow. WOW, what a noise—*schnork-phew, schnork-phew, schnork-phew*. Where's a set of earplugs when you need them?

And if Spencer's snorting—it was really snoring but sounded more like snorting—wasn't enough, the big, yellow, hundred-year-old house had its own nighttime noises. There were creepy creaking and rattling sounds, and for all I knew the place could have been haunted. As I pulled Grandma's quilt up to cover my ears I thought about how I missed our little house on the Army base in Killeen. I knew every sound and every corner of that house.

Then there was the root beer problem—I drank too much of it at dinner. And I had a root beer float just before I went to bed. Then I drank a glass of water after I brushed my teeth. Mom had warned me about drinking too much before bed, but I didn't listen. I wasn't a little kid like Spencer.

Now everyone was asleep, and the only two bathrooms in the creepy, noisy, yellow, hundred-year-old house were downstairs. I could hardly stand the thought of wandering out into the dark, creaky house. And even though I was eleven and a half years old, I knew that if I fell asleep in my current state, I was certain to wake up a soggy-dog by morning—*not* a pleasant picture!

The horrible thought of Snortin' Spencer laughing his guts out in the morning at the sight of a wet nightgown clinging to my shivering body drove me out of my bed and down the narrow green carpeted stairs in search of the nearest bathroom.

Grandma must have known that all the root beer I drank would have to go somewhere sooner or later because there were several little white night-lights plugged in all over downstairs—I was *very* grateful for this. The last thing I needed was to be stumbling around in the dark with a full bladder.

After using the bathroom at the end of the hall, I headed back toward the stairs. Just when I was about to open the door leading upstairs, I heard something.

"Help me—please." The quiet little voice coming from somewhere behind me sent my body jumping nearly three feet in the air—or at least that's how my insides felt. It sure was a good thing I had already used the bathroom!

The eerie voice in the night was followed by a jangling sound. Then I heard it again.

"Someone . . . help me . . . please. I need to get out."

I reluctantly turned around, ready to face whatever ghost it was that liked to scare young girls in the middle of the night. I soon realized, however, that the sounds were coming from inside Grandma's hundred-year-old kitchen. After crossing my fingers, I said a quick prayer, hoping more than I've ever hoped that I wasn't about to make a close encounter with the Ghost of Kitchens Past.

"That poor cow will be bellowing before long if she isn't milked soon. Gonna wake all of Edna if someone doesn't get out there and take care of their chores!"

My wide-awake eyes were led to Nanna, holding an empty ice cream bucket and trying unsuccessfully to open the kitchen door that leads to the side of the house. I noticed that there was a dead bolt clear at the top of the door that was safely locked in place. Neither Nanna nor I—even if I wanted to—could go outside to milk a cow or even *buy* a gallon of milk at this hour. I had a feeling that this wasn't the first time my great-grandma had tried to go outside in the middle of the night.

Upon closer inspection, I realized that Nanna was dressed in her flannel nightgown, a pink floral-print housedress, an old black and orange ISU Bengals jacket, and Grandma's black rubber gardening boots. Thank goodness the door was locked—what an outfit!

I slowly entered the kitchen. "Nanna?"

My great-grandmother turned around and gave me a big smile. "Oh, Lauren, honey . . . will you go find the . . . the light-thing so we can see to milk the cow? If we don't hurry, Clara Belle's going to wake up the whole town."

"Nanna, it's me . . . Allison. It's nighttime. It's time to go to bed."

"No . . . it's time to milk Clara Belle." Nanna sounded worried.

I wasn't quite sure what to do, but I knew two things for sure. Grandma didn't have a cow, and nothing but trouble would come out of Nanna walking around—especially outside—in the middle of the night. I figured I'd better try and talk Nanna out of this idea. Mom always says I'm good at talking my way out of trouble.

"It's super late. Grandma and Mom and Spencer are already asleep." Then an idea popped into my head. "I bet all the cows in Edna are asleep too."

Nanna didn't say anything for a minute, like she was trying to make sense out of what I'd said. Finally, she spoke. "Even Clara Belle? You think she's asleep?"

"Yep." I replied with a nod, even though I really wasn't sure.

Nanna slowly let go of the doorknob with her thin, curved fingers and wandered to the kitchen table where she set the empty ice cream bucket down. After a moment she finally spoke. "I'm not sure what I should be doing right now."

"It's bedtime; it's time to go to bed." I repeated.

Nanna looked into my eyes and spoke with a soft voice. "Oh."

Her eyes soon fell back to the bucket on the table, but in that short moment when our gazes were locked, I saw something or someone familiar in Nanna's eyes. My heart even did a funny little leap inside of me—kind of like one of those déjà vu things. At that moment, something—I'm not sure what, though—seemed familiar but still cloudy, like it had earlier. I wondered what it felt like for Nanna to be so confused all the time.

My great-grandmother continued to stand next to the table like she didn't know what to do next. I couldn't exactly leave her there and head back upstairs. But I didn't want to go wake up Grandma. And being pregnant and all, Mom needed as much sleep as she could get. So I figured I'd just lead Nanna back to her bedroom and then head back to bed myself.

When I reached my hand out, Nanna slowly accepted it with hers. "Come on Nanna. Let's go to bed." Hand in hand we quietly walked to her downstairs bedroom.

After I helped Nanna take off the jacket, the

floral housedress, and the boots, I tucked her into
bed just like Mom still does for me—even though
I'm almost twelve—snuggling the comforter under
her chin.

Nanna reached out from under the covers to
take my hand and held it tight. I could have tried
to pull it away, but for some reason I didn't want
to. It made me feel nice and warm inside to help
someone who needed my help. Not only did Mom
need my help these days with her being pregnant
and all, but Nanna did too.

My great-grandmother slowly lifted my hand
to her thin lips and kissed my knuckle. "I love you,
sweetheart."

I was kind of surprised at Nanna's words. Even
though they made me feel good inside, I also felt
a little funny, like maybe I should say something
back. But it seemed weird to say "I love you." I
hadn't told anybody that I loved them for a really
long time. Not even Mom or Dad. It was just a
hard thing for me to say—kind of embarrassing.
Besides, Nanna would probably forget about it by
tomorrow.

"I'll see you in the morning, Nanna."

Nanna let go of my hand but was still looking
at me with those cloudy eyes. "Now when is Daddy
coming home?" She asked.

"I'm really not sure," I replied.

That seemed to satisfy her. "Okay, sweetheart. Now you'd better get to bed. We've got a busy day ahead of us tomorrow."

I had no clue what Nanna was talking about— but then, I figured that she didn't either. I was just glad that she was back in bed, 'cause that was where I wanted to be too.

Tip-toeing out of Nanna's room, I quietly closed the door behind me and headed back up the green carpeted stairs to the room I was sharing with Spencer. And even though my little brother was snortin' away through the holes in his face, and the old yellow house was creaking and rattling in the Idaho summer wind, I easily drifted away into the land of peaceful dreams.

4

Three Lessons

In the week I'd lived in Edna, Idaho, I'd learned three lessons. The first one is that it's never a good idea to drink a lot of root beer—or anything for that matter—just before bedtime—at least not in the big yellow house. I practically had to hike the entire length of The Oregon Trail in the middle of the night up and down the green carpeted staircase, if I needed to use the bathroom—what a pain.

The second lesson I learned was that nighttime noises heard in hundred-year-old houses aren't always what you think they might be. The following morning after my middle-of-the-night encounter with Nanna in the kitchen, Grandma explained that it wasn't unusual for my great-grandma to get up and wander around the house in the middle of the night.

"She gets her days and nights mixed up," Grandma said.

Grandma also mentioned that Clara Belle was the old cow Nanna used to milk when she was about my age.

"But why did Nanna think she had to milk Clara Belle last night?" I asked.

Grandma reached for a plate of cookies from the counter and motioned me over to the kitchen table. "Sit down, sweetie. I want to explain a few things to you about Nanna."

I sat down across from Grandma and took a cookie from the plate—chewy chocolate chip, my favorite. The kind worth eating green beans for.

"Allie, your great-grandma has Alzheimer's. Some older people like Nanna get this disease— we don't know why for sure. And there's not much that we can do about it except to continue to love and care for them. She forgets who people are, where she is, and what part of her life she's living right now." Grandma sighed and then patted my hand. "It's kind of like Nanna's living in a jumbled past . . . like a deck of cards that's all mixed up and backward."

"Does Nanna really think she's a little girl again? Is that why she thought she needed to milk the cow?" I asked.

"It's not that Nanna thinks she's a little girl. Her memory just isn't the same. It's often hard for her to remember something that happened only a few minutes earlier. But Nanna still remembers many things from her childhood—like milking Clara Belle when she was about your age. Did you know it was Nanna's responsibility to milk that cow every single morning and night for years and years?"

"No wonder she remembers Clara Belle so well. I think I would have liked milking a cow every day. I like animals. That would be a fun chore."

Grandma just smiled as she took a bite of her chewy, chocolate chip cookie.

"When we lived in Killeen, it was my job to unload the dishwasher every morning. I hate unloading the dishwasher."

"How would you like to have a job around here?" Grandma asked. "Help me out a little bit around this big, old place."

I scrunched up my nose. "You want me to

unload the dishwasher?" I asked with a sense of dread.

"Naw—that's boring." Grandma said with a wave of her hand. "I don't have any cows to milk, but how about you help me by taking out food scraps to the chicken coop each day—and then you can gather the eggs while you're at it."

Now, that sounded fun!

But I was wrong—very wrong.

This is where I learned my third lesson.

Some goats actually think they are watchdogs— or at least one particular scruffy brown goat with a black beard did. That crazy goat would pace back and forth outside of the chicken coop every day, just waiting for me to feed the chickens their scraps and gather up the eggs so he could chase me around Grandma's backyard, which was more like a field.

Maybe the goat thought I was a wolf or something, trying to steal Grandma's chickens or eggs. Maybe he just didn't like humans—but that didn't make sense because the crazy thing seemed to love Grandma. Whenever she went out back the silly goat would follow her around like a little lost puppy. And Grandma said his favorite thing was to be scratched behind his ears. I'm surprised ol' Abe didn't bark and play fetch.

Well, I'd had about enough of that crazy Mr.

Abraham Lincoln. I was tired of being chased and bullied by a dumb goat. I could remember several years ago back in Killeen when a girl named Kelly Harrison wouldn't quit pulling my ponytail and calling me "Allie-gator Clay-face." (I know, pretty lame as far as name-calling goes.) I really wanted to punch her in the nose and call her "Smelly-Kelly Hairy-Legs"—now there's a great name-calling name!

But I didn't.

From somewhere I'd remembered hearing the phrase, "kill 'em with kindness." Well, I figured that I ought to give this method a try before I started punchin' people's noses. After all, they might punch back!

So the next day, even before school started, I gave Kelly Harrison an envelope with a card that I'd made all by myself at home the night before. It was a poem (remember, I'm good at talking— and writing—my way out of trouble), and it said, "Roses are red, elephants are gray, who wants to fight, when it's funner to play!" And just in case Kelly didn't like poetry, I also put a little bag of fruit snacks from my lunch into the envelope.

Then, when it was time for recess, I asked Kelly if she wanted to go swing. At first she looked a little surprised, but you know what? She said she wanted to! I don't think anyone had ever really *wanted* to play with Kelly Harrison, and I think she was a little shocked that I did—or at least I was willing to give it a try.

For the rest of that year, Kelly Harrison never again pulled my ponytail or called me Allie-gator Clay-face. And I never had to punch anyone in the nose.

But at the moment, there was a certain goat that I was *really* losing my patience with. So once again I decided to try the "kill 'em with kindness" method that had worked so well with Kelly Harrison.

Now, I really didn't figure that a goat would appreciate poetry that much. But I'd heard somewhere that "music sooths the wild beast" and since music is actually a form of poetry and Abe was definitely in the "wild beast" category—at least I thought so—I decided to write a song to sing for him on my way to the chicken coop.

Next, I decided that the "feeding" strategy of making friends would work really well, so I picked out all the decent looking vegetables from the chicken scraps and set them aside for Abe.

That evening when I opened the gate to Grandma's back lawn, I looked around for that crazy goat, and there he was as usual . . . standing guard in front of Grandma's chicken coop. After reaching up to make sure Dad's baseball cap was secure on my head (I was hoping it would help me

be brave, like my dad), I didn't waste any time and
started singing my song.

*"Allie had a little goat, little goat, little goat. Allie
had a little goat, his hair was scruffy and brown."*

Abe's ears perked up at the sound of my voice
(just like a puppy dog), but he stood his ground.
I guess he was waiting for me to make my next
move.

I was ready.

From my bucket of vegetable scraps I pulled
out a big piece of broccoli (not from my plate
though—we'd had chocolate brownies for dessert
that night). I held out the green stalk in front of my
body as I slowly walked toward the chicken coop
and started in on my second verse. I was feeling
pretty good.

*"Everywhere that Allie went, Allie went, Allie went.
Everywhere that Allie went, the goat would follow her
around."*

Actually, the song wasn't far from the truth.
If I had replaced the word "follow" with the word
"chase," I pretty well would have had things
between me and Abe explained.

This was as far in the song as I had written
words, so when I approached the chicken coop, and
"Abe, the watch-goat," with my stalk of broccoli—
which I also considered a weapon—I began to
make up more words to the song.

"He followed her to the chicken coop" (I was almost there), *"to the chicken coop"* (ten more feet), *"to the chicken coop"* (Even Kelly Harrison would be impressed). *"He followed her to the chicken coop—"*

Abe suddenly lowered his scruffy brown head and stomped one hoof.

In that split second I realized that goats couldn't care less about poetry and singing. And this particularly crazy goat probably *hated* broccoli—who could blame him for that? I wasn't about to.

In the time that it took to half-holler, half-sing *"This goat must really hate me!"* I had dropped the broccoli and bucket of chicken scraps and nearly even lost Dad's black baseball cap as I ran for my life back to the gate with a crazy brown goat named Abraham Lincoln (who thought he was a watch-dog) inches from my rear.

That night, without being asked, I unloaded the dishwasher.

● ● ● ● ●

Hey Cracker Jack,

I was so happy to receive your e-mail. Since phone calls are expensive and letters take so long, this will be the best way to stay in touch, though I'm looking forward to receiving the letter you sent.

I'm so relieved that you made it to Edna safely. And

thanks for telling me about everyone. You'll have to give Mom and Spencer a big hug for me . . . and Grandma and Nanna too. I know it's very different for you living in that big old house with Nanna and sharing a room with Spencer. I wish I could be there with you too. I sure do hate missing an entire year of your life. Maybe if we stay busy the time will pass quickly. I'm working really hard here in Baghdad, and much of my work is inside an office where it's safe. I hope that helps you feel a little better about me being here.

I love you so much, Allie. And don't worry . . . I could never forget my Cracker Jack girl—I have a great memory!

Love, Dad

5

Smells

The best thing about waking up at Grandma's house was the smell—or should I say smells. You know, those breakfast kind of smells that Grandmas seem to be the best at creating.

Grandma didn't believe in eating breakfast from a cereal box—"Too expensive," she'd say. So every morning since arriving in Idaho, my nose was treated to the smell of bacon and eggs, banana pancakes, or maybe blueberry muffins. Grandma even managed to make sticky old oatmeal smell good by adding a little cinnamon and brown sugar. But the breakfast smell I loved the very best happened when Grandma made pancakes with maple syrup.

Somehow that incredible breakfast smell even managed to creep all the way up those green carpeted stairs and into my bedroom, where I'd be sleeping as peaceful as a frog on a log. The scent of maple syrup knew how to knock on my sleeping nose and wake me right up.

But there was another reason—a more important reason—that I liked the maple syrup smell. Back home in Killeen, Texas, whenever Dad took his turn cooking—which really wasn't all that often—he always made pancakes with maple syrup. This was his "specialty," he'd say. And it didn't even matter if he was making breakfast or dinner—pancakes with maple syrup was the only item on the menu when Dad was the chef. (I bet it was the *only* thing he knew how to make.)

As I wandered barefoot down the stairs, I couldn't help but think of Dad all the way over in Iraq. I wondered how often he thought about his little family living in Edna, Idaho, while he was away. I wondered if there were any smells in Iraq that reminded him of me—like pancakes and maple syrup reminded me of him.

Thoughts of Dad quickly shifted to thoughts of Dad's baseball cap. Panic suddenly seized my chest as I searched my memory, wondering where I might have left it. How could I possibly forget something as important as my dad's favorite baseball cap? Maybe *I* was catching Old-Timers.

Then I remembered. Last night we'd watched a video in the living room. It had been warm so I took the baseball cap off and set it on the coffee table.

Without a second thought, I raced into the living room where Nanna, as usual, was sitting in her pink cushioned rocking chair wearing a sweater over a floral housedress. And there was Dad's baseball cap, right where I'd left it. I quickly picked it up and pulled it on, hoping it would cover my messy hair that I hadn't had a chance to brush yet.

The television was tuned into the morning news program, but my great-grandma seemed more interested in looking out the big picture window. The news guy was talking about the weather, and I wondered if he would start talking about Iraq soon—those news people *always* talk about Iraq. A part of me wanted to hear all about this faraway place where my dad was living for a year. But another part of me wanted to run out of the room. Sometimes I just didn't want to hear.

The things I heard and the pictures I saw scared me—made me worry about Dad, even though he said he was working in an office where it was safer. I wished he was back home.

How had I managed to live eleven and a half years never hearing about a country called Iraq, and now it seemed to bang on my ears every single day? I guess I'd heard about a city called Baghdad. But for some reason I imagined it as a place in a book where there were genies in magic bottles and flying carpets. How bad could it be?

A part of me wished that I was Spencer's age and could believe in flying carpets and genies and magic bottles. Maybe somewhere in Iraq, Dad could find a magic bottle with a genie inside to grant him three wishes. Would he wish to come home to his family? My heart told me he would if he had the choice. But I also knew that Dad took his responsibilities as a soldier seriously—he said he had a *very* important job.

But I wasn't five anymore. And even though I knew what *my* wishes would be, there were no magic bottles and no genies.

I reached up and straightened my baseball cap again. If I couldn't have Dad here with me, at least I had his favorite cap.

When I looked over at Nanna, I realized she was smiling at me. With all my thoughts of Dad and Iraq, her warm smile felt like sunshine on a cold day. Somehow this made me feel better—helped me not to worry so much.

"Good Morning, Nanna."

"Oh, Mary, I was wondering where you went."

I didn't know who Mary was, but Nanna often got people confused. Sometimes she'd even call Grandma "Nurse" or "Mamma" even though Grandma was really Nanna's only daughter. I decided not to worry about it. So what if she always called me the wrong name. I knew deep down in my heart that she still loved me—I could see it in her eyes and feel it in my heart.

"How are you doing this morning, Nanna?" I asked as I approached her chair.

Nanna didn't seem to hear my question. "Will you tell Mamma that I'd like pancakes for breakfast. I can smell them all the way in here."

"Sure," I replied. I figured she was talking about Grandma when she said "Mamma." Boy, this could get confusing if you weren't good at figuring things out. Thank goodness I was—I had to be, living with Spencer, the animal-boy.

As I walked out of the living room and approached the kitchen, I could see Grandma's back—it looked like she was flipping pancakes at the stove. Then I turned to face the table.

If it weren't for the trouble I knew was certainly

coming, I'm sure I would have laughed my pants off. Spencer, that goofball brother of mine, was apparently pretending to be a dog, or maybe even a pig, as he buried his face in the plate in front of him and began gobbling up pancakes like a half-starved animal.

"Spencer James Claybrook—" Apparently Grandma had just discovered Spencer the pig-dog. "Use your fork, for Pete's sake." Then Grandma's voice softened a bit as she set the pancake plate down on the table, folded her arms, and stared at my little brother, whose eyes were wide and nose was dripping with sticky brown syrup. Grandma almost looked like she wanted to smile.

"Sweetie, where are your manners?"

Spencer just stared at Grandma all bug-eyed and sticky-nosed as she continued her speech.

"I may have a coop full of chickens and a little goat out back, but the inside of my house isn't a barnyard, my kitchen certainly isn't a pigpen, and you, young man, are definitely not a little pig."

Spencer picked up his fork, looked at Grandma, and then let out a great big pig snort. This time Grandma *did* laugh. "You can snort like a pig all you want, but use your fork." Grandma walked over to Spencer and wiped the sticky syrup from his nose with the corner of her red and white checkered apron. This made Spencer snort even louder.

I was still standing in the entryway of the kitchen, but somehow with all of the excitement I'd forgotten about Nanna calling me Mary and wanting Grandma to bring her pancakes. I'd forgotten about everything but how great it felt to be laughing—Spencer had a way of doing that to me.

Grandma looked my way for the first time, realizing I was there.

"Good morning, sunshine. Why don't you sit down and have yourself a pancake with maple syrup?"

Well, I thought this sounded like a terrific idea—and so did my rumbling belly—so I sat next to my little piglet-of-a-brother while Grandma served us some perfectly round and fluffy golden-brown pancakes while removing my hat in the process.

"No hats at the table." Grandma had her rules and there was no arguing about them.

Just as I was taking my first bite, Mom slowly came into the kitchen with her hair still wet, face white, and eyelids heavy. She walked to the refrigerator and stared at the magnets on the door for a while before finally pulling it open.

Mom looked terrible. Sick and terrible. How could a new baby possibly be worth all of this? And the crazy part was that Mom is always this sick when she's pregnant—at least that's what she said. So why would she want another baby if it makes her so sick getting there? Maybe Mom was getting Old-Timers too and losing her memory.

"When did you start refrigerating your phone, Mother?" Mom almost managed a smile as she held up the cordless phone for Grandma to see.

"So *that's* where she put it." Grandma said as she took the phone from Mom and returned it to its proper place. "Nanna's pretty good at playing hide and seek. She can't remember where anything goes. I've found car keys in the dishwasher and toilet paper in the bread box. So unless you want to go on a treasure hunt, you'll want to keep anything important put away."

Mom closed the refrigerator door and drifted to the table.

"You need to eat something, Lauren," Grandma said as she placed a pancake onto Mom's plate.

"I know, I know. I just don't think I can," Mom replied. She placed her hand on her stomach and slouched in the chair. Mom's tummy was still flat, and it was so hard for me to believe that there actually was a little baby growing inside of it.

"They're yummy," Spencer tried to say with a mouthful of pancake.

At least he was using his fork and trying to speak with words instead of snorts. I guess he'd given up the pig routine—thank goodness for that.

"I bet they *are* good." Mom replied, but her weary expression didn't really look convinced.

Grandma came over to the table and placed her hand on Mom's shoulder. "Lauren, you need to start gaining some weight—for the baby's sake. Why, I'd say that you've even lost weight since you've been here."

"Nothing smells good, Mom—especially not pancakes with maple syrup."

"Oh, Grandma!" I blurted out, even surprising myself. "I forgot. Nanna wants some pancakes for breakfast too. She told me just before I came in here."

"Nanna finished her breakfast fifteen minutes ago," Grandma replied.

"Maybe she's still hungry," I added.

"I doubt it, honey." Grandma came around the table, poured a glass of orange juice, and held it out in front of Mom. "Nanna just forgets."

Mom reached out to take the orange juice from Grandma, took a small sip, and then set the cup down.

Grandma continued. "The person we need to be concerned about when it comes to eating is your mom."

"Mother . . . I'm trying." Mom said as she placed

one elbow on the table and picked up her fork with the other. She didn't look well at all.

"Why don't you feel good, Mom?" I asked, even though I knew the answer.

"It's the smell—I can't stand the smell of most foods right now. It was the same when I was pregnant with both you and Spencer." Mom jabbed at her pancake with her fork before taking a small bite.

Grandma looked satisfied now that Mom had started eating so she walked over to the sink and began rinsing some dishes.

As I sat watching Mom poking at her pancake and looking so miserable, it made me think about smells like I never had before. I don't think I'd ever really stopped to think very seriously about smells—never really had a good reason to. Aside from realizing that skunks and babies knew how to make quite a stink, what more did I need to know?

Funny thing is—I never knew a simple little smell like pancakes with maple syrup could do so many different things to so many different people.

6

Penny Pickett

On Friday, Mom and Grandma had to take Nanna to a doctor appointment all the way in some place called Pocatello. Nanna wasn't sick or anything—well, other than the Old-Timers—it was just a regular check-up. So me and Spencer were dropped off at Trudy Pickett's house so Spencer could play and I could finally meet her daughter.

Trudy Pickett had been Mom's best friend ever since their first day of kindergarten at Edna Elementary School, like a million years ago. I bet it was fun for Mom to have a best friend all those years. I'd had a lot of good friends back in Killeen, Texas (I'm not sure if I'd count Kelly Harrison in that group). And I'd always *wanted* a best friend— someone you could tell all your secrets to and know they'd stay secret. Someone you could have sleepovers with and pass notes to in class. But I had to move. And now I'd have to start all over again—sheesh. Lately I would have settled for just someone my age to talk to that didn't snort or bark at me, chase me around the backyard, or call me by the wrong name. I wanted a good friend like Mom's friend, Trudy Pickett.

Mom had told Spencer and me that Trudy Pickett had a ten-year-old daughter named Penny and a dog named Buster. It wasn't perfect, but it seemed like a pretty good playmate match. And even though Penny Pickett was a whole year younger than me, I'd give it a try. What other choice did I have besides hanging out with Spencer and a dog?

When we arrived at Penny Picket's house, the first greeting we received was from a big, brown, scruffy-looking dog with a curled up black tail that couldn't seem to stop swishing back and forth.

"Buster! You come sit down over here *right now!*"

I heard the voice before I actually saw the face, and I learned soon enough that it belonged to Penny Pickett. She had a strong voice, full of power and command, and I wasn't the only one to think so. Spencer immediately pulled back his little hand that was eager to pet Buster.

The dog whipped his big furry body around, nearly knocking my little brother over in the process. And before I could even say *Penny Pickett Picked a Peck of Pickled Peppers*—I'd wanted to say that out loud since the minute I heard her name was Penny Pickett—Buster was sitting at the feet of the smallest ten-year-old girl I had ever seen.

Penny Pickett had golden blond hair that was scooped up real tight into a ponytail on top of her head and tied with a fat, pink ribbon. And aside from the hair and her deep blue eyes, Penny was pink . . . *all* pink. It looked like she'd fallen into a pool of that medicine I always had to take when I was a little kid and got an ear infection. She wore a pink vest over a pink shirt. Her shorts were a slightly lighter shade of that medicine. And her bare feet were spotted at the end of each toe with shiny hot pink toenails.

I guess I didn't realize I was staring until Penny pointed it out. "What's wrong? Don't they have dogs in Texas?" She must not have realized that I was staring at her and all that pink, not at Buster.

Penny's question about dogs was probably the most ridiculous thing I'd ever heard—even from a ten-year-old. I was tempted to point this out to her but I'd promised Grandma and Mom that I'd be on my best behavior, so I just answered the ridiculous question the best way I knew how.

"There are lots of dogs in Texas. Even more than there are in Idaho . . . tons more." Honestly, I didn't know if anyone had ever counted the number of dogs in Idaho and the number of dogs in Texas to know which state had the most. But since I knew that Texas was the largest state in the continental United States (I learned that from Mrs. Halberg) and there were a bunch more people there than here in Idaho, I was taking an educated guess. (I learned about "educated guessing" from Mrs. Halberg too.) Certainly, there must be more dogs in Texas—it only made sense.

I guess I sounded convincing because Penny seemed satisfied. I was relieved because I really *did* want to have a friend here in Edna—even if she asked dumb questions once in a while. And until school started in the fall, unless I wanted to hang out with a goat that hated me, or my little brother who annoyed me and tried to steal my baseball cap,

Penny Pickett was looking like my best hope.

Spencer started petting Buster again and I was trying my hardest to think of something interesting to say. Maybe something about how pretty the color of pink is—Penny would certainly like a conversation about the color pink. But Penny's voice broke into my thoughts.

"Follow me."

I didn't ask questions; I just followed. So did Buster and Spencer. When we all started to walk, I wondered for a moment if maybe she had only wanted Buster to follow her instead of me and my brother. But then Penny began talking to me as we headed through her living room and kitchen and out the back door.

"My mom says your dad's a soldier."

"Yeah, he's in the army." I replied. "He's in Iraq for a year."

"My dad's a plumber," said Penny. "He fixes toilets and sinks and stuff like that."

"Hmmmm," was all I said, but I was really thinking how icky it would be to try and fix someone's toilet. On the other hand, I think I'd rather have Dad here in Edna fixing toilets than in Iraq away from our family for a whole year. Plus, I worried that it might be dangerous there.

Mom never actually came out and said it was dangerous in Iraq—she probably didn't want to scare me—but I could tell from the news reports that were always on the TV and radio. Mom and Grandma would turn the TV off whenever I came into the room so I knew they didn't want me to see it. But sometimes I'd just stand quietly near the door and listen—listen to mobs of men hollering and pumping their fists, listen to the gunfire snapping and popping in the air, listen to Mom crying into her hands, listen to my heartbeat pounding in my ears.

It didn't take long to learn the sounds of danger.

Penny continued on. "Dad's the only plumber in town, so he's real busy."

I wondered if maybe my dad could come back to Edna and work with Penny's dad since he was always so busy. How dangerous could fixing a toilet be?

Once the four of us were outside, Buster took off running across the green lawn with Spencer following close behind. Penny finally stopped walking when we reached the swing set and plopped down on one of the seats.

"Come over here and swing." She didn't ask me; she just told me. Sheesh, this Penny Pickett girl could be so bossy. I walked over to the swing set—but only because I *wanted* to swing.

"When my dad comes home tonight we're going

out for pizza. We do every Friday night. Dad calls it our tradition. Mom calls it her night off."

"We have traditions in my family too." I replied. I wanted her to know that I had a family as good as hers.

"Really?" said Penny. "Like what?"

"Like whenever my dad cooks a meal it's always pancakes with maple syrup." Penny didn't look impressed. I guess she figured going out to pizza was better than eating pancakes. I wasn't so sure. I'd give up pizza for a year if I could just sit down at a table with my dad for even one meal and eat pancakes with maple syrup.

Penny started swinging high, so I did the same as I thought harder about our traditions. Suddenly an image flashed in my mind.

"Oh . . . and every year, a few days after Thanksgiving, we all go to a Christmas tree farm outside of Killeen and cut down a real tree. Dad always lets me and Spencer help him saw it down." I couldn't help but smile at the memory. "Mom always takes pictures, and we drink hot chocolate with marshmallows when we're done."

"So what ya gonna do this Christmas with your dad gone and your mom having a baby?"

Why did Penny Pickett have to be nosey and ask so many questions? This was the first time since we'd been in Edna that I'd even thought as far away as Christmas. What *would* we do? How would we—how *could* we—get a Christmas tree without Dad? What would we do about our family traditions? How could we possibly be a family that still had traditions when Dad was all the way over in Iraq?

"I don't know, Penny, but can we talk about something else. How about the color pink?"

That afternoon when I went back to the big yellow house, I asked Grandma for a pencil and paper and headed upstairs. For the next hour I wrote down every Claybrook family tradition I could think of—from pancakes and Christmas trees to playing tickle-monster with Dad and eating sugar cereal on the living room floor while watching Saturday morning cartoons. Somehow, I had to save these memories. After all, I was learning a lot by living with Nanna. As much as people think their memories are locked in their brain, sometimes these memories can get lost, like with Nanna and her Old-Timers disease. I had to do my best to save our family's traditions—our memories. And I had to do it now, before *I* forgot them too.

When I first started writing I felt anxious and a little bit sad. But the more I wrote, the more I thought of Dad and our little family, and I began to feel better inside. Writing down these memories actually made me feel closer to Dad—at least in my heart. Besides, I've heard someone somewhere say that what matters most is what's in your heart. I wondered how true that was.

● ● ● ● ●

Dear Dad,

I made my first friend here in Edna. Her name is Penny Picket and she has a dog named Buster. Penny talks a lot and Buster is real friendly. Hopefully I'll make more friends when school starts. I really want to have a best friend.

I'm trying to stay busy so time will pass faster, but this isn't so easy in Edna. I feed the chickens and gather eggs every day, but first I have to get past a goat named Abe. (He doesn't like singing or broccoli, by the way.) I'd say he's smart except he thinks he's a watch dog. Crazy goat!

I wish you were here and we could eat pancakes with maple syrup together. Also, can writing letters and sending e-mail count as a tradition?

I miss you, Dad.

Love, Allie

P.S. Have you ever thought of being a plumber?

7

Secrets and Surprises

In Killeen, the mail came right to our house. But in Edna, everyone picks up their mail from little boxes inside the post office. It's kind of fun because you have to know a secret code in order to get your mail. Grandma actually called it a combination, but I preferred *secret code*. Something about the word *secret* has always been very exciting to me.

Grandma taught me the secret code to her mailbox. And since about my third day in Edna I've been walking to the little old post office every day to pick up the mail. Sometimes Grandma comes with me for the exercise, but often I just go by myself. Now, Grandma's pretty cool (as far as Grandmas go), but for no other reason I like going by myself to get away. It can be frustrating always being around people who are either irritating, pregnant, and sick, or old and forgetful. I never thought I'd say it, but I was eager for school to start.

"Are you ready to get the mail?" I asked Grandma as I entered the kitchen. She was rinsing vegetables in the sink and looked up at the clock. She shook her head slowly. "Goodness sakes. Is it ten o'clock already? Where has my morning gone?"

When I looked over at the kitchen table I noticed that Mom was sitting there, sipping from a glass of orange juice. She still looked tired and pale but maybe a little better than she had a few weeks ago. I sat down at the table next to her and took a little sip of her juice.

"Hi, Mom," I said after wiping my mouth.

Mom put a smile on her face even though I figured she didn't feel like it. "Hey there, sweetie. What are you up to?"

"I was going to see if Grandma was ready to

get the mail. Maybe there's a letter from Dad." This was my wish every day when I went to get the mail. E-mail was fun, but receiving a letter from Dad would be way cooler. And it would be nice to see his handwriting again.

"With the senior citizen's luncheon at noon, it's going to be several hours before I can break away," said Grandma as she lifted the colander full of dripping vegetables, giving it a few shakes and causing a rain storm right there in the kitchen sink.

I was about to go on my own, when Mom surprised me. "How about I walk down to the post office with you? It looks nice outside, and I think some fresh air might make me feel better." Mom slowly stood, and I wondered if she was really up to this.

We were about to walk out the door, and I turned around to ask Mom something when suddenly, I noticed *it*.

"Mom . . . you're finally getting fat!" I nearly squealed.

"It's called pregnant, Allie," Mom said as she patted the little bulge now poking out just below her belly button.

"That's what I meant." I clarified as I reached out, touching Mom's hands and stomach at the same time.

For the first time I felt the beginnings of a new little baby growing inside of Mom's stomach. It felt like a little round ball—a ball full of baby—my little brother or sister. I couldn't help but pat it. Mom didn't seem to mind. As a matter of fact, it made her laugh.

"Do you know if it's a boy or a girl yet?"

"I don't know. I guess it will have to be a surprise. But from the way I've been feeling, I'd have to think it's a girl. I felt sick like this when I was pregnant with you too." Mom poked at my stomach trying to make me laugh, but I refused. Well, at least as long as I could until I couldn't stand it anymore and gave in. It felt good to be laughing with Mom again. Since we'd been here in Edna, she'd hardly laughed at all. I think partly because she didn't feel good because of the new baby growing in her belly, but also because she missed Dad. I knew this for sure because I missed him too.

Just as we were about to walk out the kitchen door on the side of the house and head for the post office, I remembered something very important.

"Where's Dad's hat?" I said, mostly to myself as I touched the top of my head. I'd worn that baseball cap every day to the post office—for good luck, I suppose. But now as I looked around, I couldn't see it anywhere.

With a sense of urgency I ran into the entryway, but I didn't see it on Grandma's coat tree. This was where Grandma liked me to keep it when it wasn't on my head—which was hardly ever. Still, sometimes I forgot.

As I searched around the coat tree, I noticed a strange noise coming from the living room. I could hear a man's voice from the television. But there was another sound—a more familiar sound. Spencer! If he had my hat again . . .

I raced into the living room to see Nanna smiling and clapping her hands at Spencer, who had his nose buried into his shoulder as he waived his arm up and down while making strange trumpeting noises. The television was tuned into a nature channel, and the show was obviously about elephants.

And there was Dad's black baseball cap—right on my little brother's big elephant head.

Without further warning, I walked over to Spencer, quickly snatched the hat from his head, and pulled it onto my own.

"Hey!" Spencer wailed.

"Dad gave this hat to *me* before he left." I reminded my little brother, pushing him back as he tried to jump up and take the hat from my head.

"He's *my* dad too." Spencer hollered and then stuck his tongue out at me.

I ignored my pesky little brother and ran back into the kitchen with Dad's black baseball cap sitting securely on my head. Now I was ready to get the mail.

When we reached the post office, a sense of excitement suddenly filled my heart. Very carefully, I turned the knob to the right, then to the left, and then right again as I found the secret code letters of Grandma's mailbox. As I pulled up on the lever, the little door opened.

When I looked in the box, there were several white envelopes stacked together, but on the very bottom was a fat brown envelope. I grabbed for the bottom one and pulled it out. It was familiar handwriting, and it was addressed to Lauren, Allie, and Spencer Claybrook.

It was a letter from Dad.

Mom noticed too because we both let out a scream right there in the middle of the Edna post office, and I started jumping up and down. Mom quickly took the envelope from my hands.

"Open it . . . open it," I squealed.

"I want to, Allie . . . but not right here. Let's hurry home and open it there, okay?" I guess I could see Mom's point. So I grabbed the rest of the mail, closed the mailbox, and the two of us hurried back to Grandma's to open the big brown envelope.

When we raced into the kitchen and Mom started tearing open the envelope, Grandma said, "Looks like we've got news from Iraq today."

"We got a letter from Dad," I clarified.

Mom pulled out several sheets of paper and a small white envelope. She held up one piece of paper. "This one's for Spencer." Then she held up the sealed envelope. "And it looks like this one is for Miss Allison Jayne Claybrook's eyes only. That's what it says right here." Mom pointed to the front of the envelope and then handed it to me.

My heart was racing, and I suddenly wanted peace and quiet. I wanted to be alone. So I took the letter from Mom's hand and ran up the green carpeted stairs into the bedroom Spencer and I shared. I was relieved that he was still in the living room imitating the animals on the television for Nanna. Thank goodness she seemed to enjoy my little brother and his silly imitations. I was tired of them, but since Nanna couldn't remember things so good, she didn't remember how annoying he could be.

After falling into the center of my bed, I carefully looked at the envelope. It *did* say, *FOR ALLISON JAYNE CLAYBROOK'S EYES ONLY!* Carefully, I ripped open the envelope and pulled out a piece of paper. I was surprised to see a twenty-dollar bill fall onto my comforter. I set the money on my pillow and looked at the letter again.

Before I started reading, I sniffed at the paper to see if I could smell anything of Dad or Iraq in the letter. I couldn't. It just smelled like plain old paper that anybody could get anywhere. But it wasn't. Just a week or so earlier Dad had held this very piece of paper in his hands and wrote a letter to me on it. This made it the most precious piece of paper in the entire universe.

As I started to read Dad's writing, it was almost as if I could hear his voice in my head. I was relieved that I could still remember the sound of it—the best sound in the world!

● ● ● ● ●

Dear Allie,

How is my girl doing? I bet you're being such a great help to Mom and Grandma. I love receiving your letters and e-mail and hearing all about life in Edna. When I close my eyes at night I can even picture in my mind all of the things you write about. That's my favorite time of the day . . . when I'm thinking about all of you.

How are Spencer and Mom? I sure do miss you three. It's hard to believe that before long we'll be a family of five. In Mom's e-mails she always says how excited you are and how you want a baby sister. I'd love to have another little girl, and if we do, I hope she turns out just like you, although nobody could ever take the place of my Cracker Jack girl.

I don't know if you remembered, but Mom's birthday is at the end of this month. Here is some money so that you and Spencer can buy her a little present. I'm sure Grandma will take you shopping if you ask.

I know you'll be a good girl and help to make this a special birthday for Mom. And since I can't be there, maybe you can help me out by writing down all that happens—you can make me a memory, since I can't be there to make one myself.

You are so special to me, Allie, and I think about you every day, especially when I see little Iraqi girls about your age. They aren't much different from you, except they speak a different language. They love their fathers, and their fathers love them too. Some things are the same no matter where in the world you are.

I love you, Cracker Jack!

Love, Dad

8

Goats and Cookies

Even though Abe the goat didn't like me, I continued to do my chore for Grandma and take food scraps out to the chickens every day while collecting eggs. And every day, the scruffy old goat chased after me like some slobbering dog—only he didn't slobber. Instead, he pointed those horns in my direction like I was some sort of bull's-eye, giving me reasons enough to run the other way.

Good thing I'm about as fast as a scared cat—not that I'm calling myself a scardey-cat. I just don't want to feel a couple of goat's horns poking my backside. Ouch!

But after a while, you get to a point in life when you just can't run anymore. It doesn't matter whether you're running from a girl like Kelly Harrison 'cause she's pulling your ponytail or a goat named Abraham Lincoln, who thinks you're swiping his eggs. And you don't stop running because your legs are tired. More like your patience is tired, and you know that it's time to face the enemy. Dad said something about that before he left. Now I knew what he meant.

At the moment, my enemy was a goat.

I'd been thinking through the whole situation with Abe, and I decided that maybe I just needed to put myself in his shoes—or hooves—if I wanted to understand him better and why he had it in for me. In the past when I'd tried to make friends with Abe, I went about it the wrong way. I'd tried to win him over with a song and food scraps—broccoli, to be exact.

But when I thought about it, I wondered—would *I* like it if someone sang to me while giving me *their* leftover vegetables? To be honest, I'd probably be even madder at them—at least about the vegetable part. I'd say, "Eat your own vegetables. I have a hard enough time trying to gag my own down so that I can have dessert."

Maybe Abe the goat felt the same way, only *he* never got dessert—ever. I could see why he was a grumpy old thing most of the time. I would be too if all I had to eat was grass and a leftover vegetable once in a while.

At that very moment, the perfect solution to all of my goat problems finally came to me.

An hour later when it was time to take out the scraps, I was prepared. In one hand I held a plastic bucket full of food scraps—nasty looking stuff, I might add. In the other; however, I had two of Grandma's chewy chocolate chip cookies. And to top it off, on my head I wore Dad's black baseball cap. This was to help me be brave in the face of danger—or should I say, Abe. I always wore that hat, but today when I put it on, I decided to pretend like I was a brave soldier, like Dad.

If Grandma's goat wasn't impressed with her chewy chocolate chip cookies, then for all I cared, the ornery critter could just continue to think he was a watch dog. And maybe I'd just have to learn how to wrestle goats. I wasn't sure there'd be another alternative besides quitting. And I wasn't about to do that. If Dad could go a million miles away to build bridges and roads, I could stand up to a stupid goat.

When I opened the gate, Abe's head jerked up from the patch of grass he'd been nibbling on. And even though he couldn't talk, I felt like I could read that goat's mind just as clear and easy as I can read Mom's mind during those certain times when she looks at me with her arms folded, lips pressed together and head shaking back and forth, all slow and steady like.

As I looked into Abe's face, I was sure that he was saying, "Hey, short human girl with the funny black thing on your head. I just dare you to walk past me and try to toss that bucket of slop that only a pig or chicken could appreciate into my coop. And I know you're fixin' to steal my chicken's eggs. Well, you'll have to get past me first. Come on . . . I dare ya."

But I was prepared. Immediately, I stuck one of the cookies in my back pocket while I held the other out with a straight arm, like a policeman showing his identification badge.

As I took a step forward, Abe, the goat, tilted his head slightly. Probably trying to figure out what in the heck I had in my hand. It certainly wasn't a leftover piece of broccoli or even a cold, soggy pancake. I was holding my all-time favorite food item in the universe. And I could only hope that goats have a good sense of smell, or at least good eyesight, 'cause for all I knew, Abe might have thought I had a rock in my hand and wanted to knock him on the head with it (actually, that might not be such a bad idea).

After taking another big step, Abe began to approach me. His walk soon turned into a trot . . . and then a run.

I had two choices at the moment. I could turn and run myself or face that dumb goat. I'd tried the first way a few dozen times already and didn't want to do it anymore. So I continued to stand tall and hold out my cookie. But I also began to holler while hopping up and down like I had pants full of fire ants. "Cookie, cookie, cookie!" I had no idea if Abe understood English, but it was worth a try.

Well, I must have startled Abe because when he was about three feet away from me, he suddenly came to a stop. Boy, was I relieved. The goat was staring at me like I was crazy or something. Probably a lot like the way I look at him every day.

I quit jumping and hollering the minute Abe quit charging, and the two of us just looked at each other until I dropped the cookie on the ground. After sniffing a few times, and obviously picking up the scent of chocolate chips, Abe took the entire cookie in his mouth and ate it—and liked it. Maybe I had a few things in common with this crazy goat after all.

I quickly took the other cookie out of my back pocket. It was a little squished and was broken into pieces, so I tossed Abe another piece on the ground and while he was busy eating, I headed for the chicken coop as fast as my feet would take me without running. By the time I'd reached the wire door, Abe had caught up to me, looking for more of the cookie.

For the first time since I'd been at Grandma's, I felt something other than fear and hatred for Abraham Lincoln, the goat. I actually respected him for knowing just what he wanted and going after it. For doing what he thought was his duty to Grandma by protecting the chicken coop.

It even made me think of Dad—but only for a minute. I wasn't out of trouble yet.

"Here you go, Abe. I hope you like it." I held out another piece of cookie and this time the goat ate it right out of my hand. His chin whiskers tickled my palm.

Reaching up, I patted Abe on the neck, and then scratched him behind the ears. Penny Picket told me that her dog Buster loved to be scratched behind the ears more than anything and I figured that if Abe really thought he was a watch dog then he'd probably love it too.

I think he did.

● ● ● ● ●

Dear Dad,

I finally made friends with Abe, the goat. But if we ever get a pet, I think I'd rather have a dog.

I miss you, Dad. And I also think about you at night before I fall asleep.

Love, Allie

9

The Party

Twenty dollars sure seems like a lot of money when it comes falling out at you from the insides of an envelope that's traveled all the way from Iraq. But when you're searching for something cool for your mom's birthday and you want the present to be real special, all of a sudden twenty dollars doesn't seem like so much money after all.

Grandma finally helped me pick out some pretty

stationary so Mom could write mushy love letters to Dad and some nice, peachy smelling lotion for Mom to rub on her bulging belly. It smelled so yummy; I almost wanted to eat the stuff. We also bought a big box of chocolates. Now, *that's* what I really wanted to eat. I had a feeling Mom would share, so I made sure we got my favorite kind. I tried to think of what Dad would have bought her if he were here but all that thinking started to make me sad—and mad. We wouldn't be here if Dad hadn't gone to Iraq. When I looked up at Grandma, she smiled at me. I was glad she couldn't read my mind.

My greatest wish was that the night would be special for Mom, being her thirty-fifth birthday and all. Trudy Pickett, her husband the plumber, and Penny had come over for a barbecue to celebrate.

I tried extra hard to do what I was supposed to do. I helped Grandma peel potatoes, I was nice to Spencer, and I even dressed up in clothes that I knew she liked (even though I was too old for flowered shirts). The only important thing that was missing was Dad's baseball cap. I wanted to wear it for good luck, but I couldn't find it anywhere.

It wouldn't have surprised me if Spencer had hid the hat somewhere, or wore it outside and left it in the dirt. He just didn't seem to realize how important it was. The kid was hopeless. But hat or no hat, I knew Dad would have been proud of me for helping to make Mom's birthday a special one so I tried not to think about the hat (even though I knew he was hiding it from me—he was always after my hat). I hoped again that the new baby wouldn't be a boy; I don't think I could stand it.

"You sure do look cute when you're pregnant, Lauren," said Trudy Pickett before poking another fork full of steak into her mouth. Mom's best friend since kindergarten sure didn't seem to have trouble chewing and talking at the same time. Mom always told me to chew with my mouth closed. I wondered why it was okay for Trudy to do it and not me.

"I sure don't feel cute," Mom replied. "But I'm feeling a lot better now that the baby's starting to show and I'm not so sick." Mom placed her hand on the little ball of her belly and smiled.

I wondered if just looking at her belly all poking out and knowing that my baby brother or sister was inside made Mom feel a lot better. Did looking at me and Spencer make her feel better too?

"Hey, Mom?" I tried to get her attention from across Grandma's picnic table. Trudy was talking to Mom some more, and she still had her mouth full of meat. Mom held up one finger in my direction without looking at me. That meant to wait a minute; she was busy. I'd seen that finger a bazillion times, and I hated it. When I'm a mom I'm never going to hold up my finger like that. Never.

I took a few sips of my lemonade and tried to be patient while I waited. Now I knew where Penny Pickett learned how to talk so much.

"Mom?" I said again, a little louder while Trudy was taking a quick breath. I was hoping that Trudy had finished talking. Apparently, she hadn't, but now Mom was ready to pay me some attention . . . but not the good kind.

"Allison Jayne Claybrook, it's not polite to interrupt someone while they're speaking."

I wanted to say that it also wasn't polite to speak with food in your mouth and to talk so much that no one else could even get a single little word in, but I didn't. I also didn't feel like saying anything to Mom anymore—I didn't need to. I could tell by the look on her face that staring at that poking-out little belly of hers obviously made her much happier than I did. I should have guessed.

Dad wouldn't have gotten upset with me if he were here. He would have smiled and said, "What does my Cracker Jack want?"

I really missed Dad.

Mom just sighed when I didn't say anything, and of course, Trudy started talking some more. Once again, Mom was smiling, and Trudy had put a yellow heap of potato salad into her mouth between words. It was gross, and I decided that

Mom was right about that rule after all. I just wish she'd tell it to Trudy.

I looked around at the backyard. Spencer and Penny were standing out near the back gate trying to pet Abe, who looked like he didn't trust Penny at all. I knew the look on that goat's face very well—even from far away. Grandma was taking some of the food back into the kitchen, and Mr. Pickett, the plumber, was sitting in a lawn chair working on his second helping of barbecue beans. Finally, I glanced over to the covered bench swing that faced the garden. During the summer when the weather was nice, Nanna liked to sit there and watch Grandma work in the garden. Since the bench swing had a cushioned seat and an awning that provided shelter from the sun, it was a perfect spot for Nanna to rest comfortably.

Grandma wasn't doing any gardening at the moment, but apparently she had walked Nanna out to her favorite spot. A colorful afghan covered her legs, and she wore a yellow sweater even though it felt really good outside. At the moment Nanna seemed more fun than anyone else at the party.

After making my way over to the covered swing, I found a spot next to Nanna. As I sat down, the cushioned seat made a long hissing sound like it had just let out a big, deep breath.

I did the same.

When I looked over at Nanna, she was staring out at the space in front of us, but not looking at anything in particular. Her expression was calm and her eyes looked clear—not confused, like they often did when I tried to talk to her. Sometimes when her eyes were clear, she seemed like a regular old lady—though it wasn't often. She would notice what I was wearing and call Grandma by her right name. I liked those times and hoped she wouldn't bring up Clara Belle again or start calling me by the wrong name.

I began to wonder if she even noticed that I was sitting next to her. She didn't seem to.

"Hi, Nanna. How are you doing?"

My words seemed to float away in the gentle breeze of the Idaho summer night as Nanna continued to gaze straight ahead. She was so still that I wondered if maybe she'd fallen asleep with her eyes open. My great-grandma slept a good part of the day, often sitting in her pink chair in the living room but never with her eyes open— at least not that I knew of. So much for having a conversation with her.

I wondered if I should go get Grandma, but Nanna finally spoke and her voice was even and calm. "I need to go home now." She was still looking ahead at nothing in particular, but at least I knew she was awake.

"Do you want me to help you back into the house?" I asked.

Nanna didn't respond—didn't even look at me. Maybe she was feeling a little cool from the evening breeze, even though *I* thought it felt good. Grandma always said that Nanna was quick to get a chill and that's why she always wore a sweater. I didn't want Nanna getting sick or anything, so I pulled the colorful afghan up to cover her shoulders.

When I did that, Nanna finally looked over at me, but her eyes were no longer clear.

"Who are you?" she asked.

This didn't surprise me; I was used to it now. Sometimes Nanna called me Lauren—that's my mom's name. Other times she thought I was her sister Mary who died a long time ago. She never called me Allie. The Old-Timers disease had stolen her memory. It made me mad sometimes, like now. It didn't seem fair to her, or to me.

"Do you want to go back into the house?" I repeated. "Are you cold?"

Nanna looked at me for a moment with frightened eyes. Then she quickly pushed the afghan off, throwing it to the grass, and started searching around with her head and arms moving every which way as if she'd lost something and was trying to find it.

"I don't know what I'm supposed to be doing." Nanna cried and then she tried to stand up. But the rocking bench quickly shifted backward with the force of Nanna's weight and she began to loose her balance.

With every ounce of strength I had, I shot to my feet and tried to hold onto Nanna's body so she wouldn't fall, as well as steady the bench to keep it from swinging back any further. And even though Nanna was thin, I just couldn't hold her weight up. I needed help.

"Mom! Grandma! Help!" I screamed.

Before I knew it everyone, even the plumber, had arrived at the bench swing. But it was too late. Nanna and I were both on the ground now, and Nanna was crying like a little girl. I was worried for a minute that someone might think that I'd been mean to her or made her fall, but when I tried to explain, I started to cry.

"I didn't do anything. She tried to stand and lost her balance. I was trying to hold her up, but I . . ."

Mom pulled me into her arms while Grandma and Trudy tried to calm Nanna. She screamed when they tried to pick her up, so Grandma told Mr. Pickett to call an ambulance.

"Shhhhh," Mom whispered into my ear. I continued to sob into her chest. "Everything'll be okay. This kind of thing can happen with elderly people. It's no one's fault."

I wanted to believe Mom, but I felt so awful. As I continued to soak my tears into her shirt, she lifted my chin and looked into my eyes.

"I love you, Allison. And Grandma and Nanna love you too. This was just an accident." I could see the love in Mom's eyes, but my heart was still hurting. I was afraid for Nanna having to ride in an ambulance and go to the hospital.

"But . . . ," I tried to talk but Mom placed her finger on my lips, and then began to wipe the moisture from my cheeks as she spoke.

"It could have been me or Spencer sitting there with Nanna . . . but it just happened to be you. You're the one who was thoughtful enough to keep her company."

Nothing more was said as Mom walked me, Spencer, and Penny into the house and put a video on for us so we'd be out of the way when the ambulance came. Grandma, Trudy, and Mr. Pickett went to the hospital with Nanna and for the first time since I'd been in Edna, I had a sleepover. Penny Pickett stayed the night at the big yellow house and she kept me up for hours talking nonstop. I was beginning to wonder if I really wanted a best friend.

All night long I kept reliving the whole incident

with Nanna falling. It was like a bad nightmare that wouldn't quit. The only thing that seemed to make me feel better was remembering Mom's words, "I love you, Allison . . . and Nanna loves you too."

10

Making Memories

When I woke up on Sunday morning, I found out that Nanna would be staying in the hospital for a while. I learned that when she fell from the swing, she broke her hip and had to have surgery. I really felt awful about this. I wished I hadn't gone and sat by her. Then everything would be fine right now, and Nanna would be sitting in her pink rocker instead of at the hospital.

"Will I be able to go and see her?" I asked as Mom, Spencer, and I ate our oatmeal at the kitchen table. Grandma was still asleep. She'd been at the hospital most of the night and needed the rest—not great news for me and Spencer, since Grandma's oatmeal always tasted so much better than Mom's.

"Maybe in a few days, honey," said Mom. "Right now the doctor has her on some pretty strong pain medicine that makes her sleepy most of the time."

"Is Nanna gonna die?" Spencer asked, and I wondered where that thought came from.

Mom took a deep breath before answering. "Nanna's not going to die from a broken hip, buddy. But she will probably die someday. She's very old, and her body is worn out."

My little brother furrowed his eyebrows, scrunched up his nose, and slapped his spoon in the bowl of uneaten oatmeal.

"I don't *want* Nanna to die. She's the only one who likes it when I pretend to be an elephant . . . or a dog . . . or some other animal."

I guess he had a point. No one could make Nanna smile like Spencer. Maybe because he didn't expect her to call him by the right name. The two of them seemed to have an interesting connection.

Mom put her arm around Spencer and gave him a hug. "You sure do know how to make her smile," said Mom, pulling him in close. "I don't think it will happen too soon, but we really don't know for sure."

We all sat quietly, looking at our not-very-yummy oatmeal, when a great idea popped into my mind. "Mom, since we can't visit Nanna, do you think we can make her a present? Something to make her smile."

"Yeah," Spencer squealed. "I want to draw her a picture of an elephant. Nanna loves elephants."

"That's a wonderful idea," said Mom.

"We should draw things that will remind her of us and of home."

"Yeah!" Spencer squealed.

For the remainder of the morning, my little brother and I kept busy creating pictures and cards to hang up on Nanna's hospital room wall.

Since I was already drawing pictures for Nanna, I decided to draw some for Dad as well—make him some memories since he couldn't be here to make the memories himself.

I drew two pictures of the big yellow house— one for Dad and one for Nanna. To get it right, I actually sat out on the lawn with my paper and colored pencils like a real artist. I knew Dad would love the picture. I wasn't sure about Nanna, but I could hope.

Then, I drew another picture for Nanna—a

cow with a girl standing next to it holding a pail. Maybe drawing these pictures would actually help Nanna's Old-Timer's disease—help her remember things better. I wondered why the hospital could fix her hip but not her memory.

When I examined Spencer's pictures, I knew what the first picture was immediately—an elephant. But I was a little puzzled about the second drawing. It was mostly green except for what I could only guess were people. There were several other weird splotches as well.

"What are those?" I pointed to the splotches.

Spencer took in a deep breath and then let it blow out through noisy, fluttering lips. "Can't you see? They're Grandma's chickens."

"Oh . . . of course," I replied, trying to sound serious, but I couldn't help turning away and laughing to myself. Then I pointed to the brown thing with four legs. If I hadn't known better, I would have guessed it was a dog. Maybe even Penny Pickett's dog, Buster. But since Grandma doesn't have a dog—at least not a *real* one. I took the most obvious guess.

"This must be Abe."

"Yep!" Then my little brother began pointing to the other things in his drawing—presumably people. "And this is Grandma, and this is Mom, and this is you, and this is me."

I couldn't help but notice the last figure—the one he said was himself. It was wearing Dad's black baseball cap—the one he gave to *me* before he left for Iraq. And that reminded me that I hadn't seen my hat for two whole days. I could only imagine who was hiding it.

"Where did you put my hat?" I asked, mad that I'd forgotten about it and wanting him to know how serious I was about getting it back—now!

Spencer was still examining his masterpiece. "I'm wearing it right here," he said, pointing to the black splotch with a line sticking out.

I grabbed the picture away from him and held it high above my head.

"Hey ... gimme my picture back. It's not for you. It's for Nanna."

"I'll give it back when you tell me where you hid my hat."

Spencer tried to jump up and grab the picture, but I was too tall. "Gimme my picture!"

"Give *me* my hat," I demanded.

"It's not your hat ... it's Dad's."

"Dad gave it to *me!* Now you'd better tell me where it is or I'm going to throw your picture away."

Spencer began to cry. "I don't have the hat. I didn't do anything with it. Gimme back my picture."

Mom came to see what was happening just as I threw his silly, splotchy, picture on the ground and stomped out of the room. I really wouldn't have thrown the picture away. I just wanted to scare him into thinking I would. I *had* to find Dad's hat, and I knew the little dweeb must be hiding it somewhere.

Mom yelled after me but I ran to my room and slammed the door. Everything in my life was going wrong and I didn't know how to fix it.

● ● ● ● ●

Dear Allison,

In Mom's e-mail this morning she told me all about what happened with Nanna. Are you okay? I'm sorry I can't be there right now to give you a big hug. Sometimes it's hard to understand why we end up in certain places at certain times when things don't seem to be going how we'd like them to. It's at these times that we must stay close to the ones we love, and who love us . . . even if it can only be through letters and memories.

I hope you always remember how much I love you!

Love, Dad

11

Memories, Past and Present

Most of the time, life is full of the same old stuff: the same house, the same school, the same friends, even the same old peanut butter and jelly sandwiches for lunch—it's a good thing I really like peanut butter and jelly.

But then, without warning, life can get kind

of crazy and nothing is the same anymore. That's how the last few months have been for me. I was finally getting used to all the new things in my life like living in Edna, Idaho, at Grandma's big yellow house, and Nanna's Old-Timer's disease, and friends like Penny Pickett and a pet goat named Abe, and not having Dad around, when suddenly, things got all crazy again.

Grandma had spent the last two days at the hospital and only came home to sleep. I hadn't even seen her since she left with Nanna in the ambulance. So when she called, I was anxious to find out if she'd put our pictures on Nanna's hospital room wall, and if Nanna liked them.

But the only thing Mom said to Grandma on the phone was, "Uh-huh . . . uh-huh," over and over. I kept trying to whisper, "Ask Grandma if Nanna likes our pictures," but Mom waved me off and walked in another direction as she continued her "uh-huhs."

When she finally got off the phone, I was watching cartoons with Spencer. We'd been laughing at the show, but as soon as I saw Mom's face, I didn't feel like laughing anymore.

Mom walked over to the television and turned it off.

"Hey . . . " Spencer howled, but Mom ignored his complaining.

"That was Grandma calling from the hospital." At that point even Spencer realized that maybe he'd better hush up and listen. The quiet in the room suddenly seemed awful loud.

I was afraid to ask the question buzzing in my head but couldn't resist. "Is Nanna going to be okay?"

Mom sat down between the two of us on the couch and put her arms out so we would scoot in next to her.

"I don't think so, honey. Her body is just too old and frail. The doctors told Grandma that the surgery was hard on Nanna. She hasn't reacted well to the medications."

"But can't they fix her at the hos-ti-pull?" Spencer's forehead was creased in worry.

"They've been trying, buddy." Mom kissed the top of Spencer's head and then continued. "Nothing seems to be working." There was more loud silence before Mom spoke again. "The doctor told Grandma that Nanna's probably not going to last much longer."

"Can't they try harder?" I asked, but my heart already knew the answer.

Spencer suddenly pulled his body away from Mom and hopped to his feet. "Nanna *can't* die!" He ran from the room, and we could hear the screen door in the kitchen slam.

I looked up at Mom, and her eyes were wet with tears.

My stomach began to ache in an empty sort of way. "She's going to die . . . isn't she?"

Mom didn't say anything, just nodded her head. I was glad when she pulled me in close. I held tight onto Mom—so tight that I felt like I was holding onto our little baby as well. I didn't want to ever let go. I just wanted to know that she'd always be there with me—that she'd never leave.

We sat with our arms around each other for a little while longer until Mom leaned back so I could look into her face.

"I need to go find Spencer now." Mom stood up, walked out of the living room and then out of the house leaving me alone in the quiet.

I'd been so mad for so long, and now it seemed silly. I loved Nanna. Even though she never called me by my real name, somehow she had become one of my favorite parts of Edna, Idaho. Now she would be gone, and I'd never even told her that I loved her.

I thought of all the things I'd learned about her childhood, like Clara Belle, and her sister Mary, and how she loved and missed her dad—he was the one who had built this old house. These were all of Nanna's happy memories—the things she remembered.

For a moment, I wondered what Spencer or Mom would remember if they ever got the Old-Timers disease. Would they ever think about me? I started to cry as I realized they probably wouldn't. With the way I'd been acting all summer, I just might be the first thing they'd forget.

As I looked around the room full of Grandma's furniture and decorations, it felt empty, like my heart. Nanna usually spent most of her days sitting in the pink-cushioned rocker. But she never would again. And the only thing left to remind me that she'd even been there was a white sweater draped across the back of the rocker. Nanna always wore a sweater.

I walked over to the chair and picked up the sweater. When I brought it close to my face, the smell of Nanna's lilac lotion made me feel like she was right there with me, even though I knew she really wasn't.

As I walked toward her bedroom to put the sweater away, I couldn't resist sliding it around my shoulders. I knew it would be too big for me, but I really wanted to wear it—just for a minute. My hands were lost in the long sleeves, but to me it felt like a perfect fit. Like a hug from someone you love.

Nanna's bedroom really wasn't very small; it just felt that way because it was so full. There was a lot of furniture in there, but the room was also full of memories. Some couldn't actually be seen—only felt. Like my memory of tucking Nanna into her bed on the first night we'd arrived in Edna when I'd found her in the kitchen, and she'd wanted to go out back in the middle of the night and milk a cow.

But there were memories that *could* be seen too, from Nanna's sweater around my shoulders to the pictures hanging on the walls and sitting on the dressers. I'd seen them there a million times before but never actually took the time to really look at them.

Most of the pictures were really old, and I had no idea who some of the people were. But others, I was able to figure out. In one, a young-looking Nanna—probably a teenager—was sitting on top of a horse. I'd never imagined Nanna riding a horse, but I knew that Grandma could. A lot of people in Edna rode horses. Not because they didn't have cars like in the olden days, but because it was fun. I bet Nanna taught Grandma to ride a horse like Mom taught me how to hit a tennis ball with a racket. I'm still not very good at it, but Mom said everything eventually comes with practice and patience.

Then there was another picture of Nanna. She was a little bit older than in the horse picture, and she was holding a baby. I had no idea if she was holding Grandma or some other baby. Who can tell with a baby picture? Even though I knew that Nanna was Grandma's mom, it was hard to imagine her holding babies, riding horses, or doing much of anything besides sitting in the pink rocker or maybe sitting out on the covered bench swing near the garden. I only knew the confused Nanna—the one with Old-Timer's that made her memory broken and her mind confused. The only Nanna I could remember was the one who never really knew me or remembered my name.

As I stood in the room full of Nanna's memories, embraced in her sweater and looking at her pictures, the sound of chickens woke me out of my little daydream. I'd been so busy drawing pictures for Nanna that I hadn't remembered to take out scraps or collect eggs since she fell from the swing.

I quickly pulled off the sweater and looked around, wondering where Grandma kept Nanna's sweaters. When I opened the top drawer of the tall dresser, there were only socks and underwear. I should have figured. That's the same drawer Mom has me put my socks and underwear in. Since I keep shirts and sweaters in the third drawer, I decided to look there.

When I opened the drawer, I was completely

in shock and totally surprised at what I saw. What in the world was Dad's black baseball cap doing inside Nanna's sweater drawer?

Then I remembered the conversation we'd had with Grandma when we first arrived in Edna. I remembered the phone in the fridge and the car keys in the dishwasher and the toilet paper in the bread box. I remembered Nanna and how she misplaced things. It was just another part of the Old-Timer's that was hard to understand.

I took the hat out of the drawer and held it in my hands but couldn't bring myself to put in on. Thoughts of me holding up Spencer's picture so he couldn't reach it and accusing him of hiding Dad's hat were fresh in my mind. I'd been so certain that I was right. Now, the only thing I was certain of was that I needed to apologize to my little brother— right away.

The screen door slammed shut again, and I figured it was Spencer until I heard Mom's voice.

"Allie . . . I can't find Spencer anywhere. I think he might have walked over to Trudy's, knowing how much he loves that dog of hers." Mom was trying to sound like she wasn't worried, but I knew she was—I could see it in her eyes. Spencer never left the big yellow house on his own. It wasn't allowed. "Will you keep looking for him around here while I drive over there really quick?"

"Sure." I replied and walked out back while Mom spun the wheels of The Bruise in the gravel of Grandma's driveway as she left for Trudy Pickett's house.

After hollering Spencer's name a few times, I noticed that Abe seemed to be pacing in front of the chicken coop. I needed to collect eggs anyway, so I figured I might as well check in there first.

Even though me and Abe had learned how to get along, Spencer was still terrified of Grandma's goat. Can't say that I blame him. I suppose that's why I was so surprised to see my little brother squatting down into a little ball inside the corner of the chicken coop.

"There you are." I nearly squealed, startling all the chickens from their afternoon naps. Spencer didn't respond—just kept his head down and his arms wrapped around his knees.

"Mom's out looking for you. She thinks you walked over to Penny Picket's to play with Buster."

Spencer still sat there all hunched over, but when I looked closely, I could see that he was crying. He wasn't making a puddle of tears or anything, but his body was shaking just a bit.

When I walked over and put my hand on my little brother's shoulder, he reached out with one hand and tried to push me away. This only made me feel worse for how I'd treated him about Dad's hat. Somehow saying sorry, especially at a time like this, just didn't seem enough.

Without saying another word, I took Dad's black baseball cap and placed it on Spencer's head. It was his now; he needed it more than me. Then I turned around, and as I headed for the chicken coop door I thought of something I wanted to say. Something I hoped would make my little brother feel better—and maybe me too.

"I love you, Spencer." It felt weird to say that to my annoying little brother who always drove me crazy. But as I said it, I realized it had been a long time since I had told anyone that I loved them. In fact, I wasn't even sure I'd said it when Dad left for Iraq. And I sure wished I'd said it to Nanna before she ended up sick and dying in the hospital.

As I began to leave the chicken coup, the chickens were startled again—this time by my brother.

"Allie!" He yelled.

When I turned around, I was nearly knocked over as Spencer ran into my arms. You know, sometimes it's not so awful giving your little brother a hug. Sometimes it can even feel pretty good.

"Will you walk me back to the house?" he asked.

"No problem." I said as I pulled the bill of his baseball cap down so it covered his eyes.

Spencer laughed through sniffles. Then he fixed his cap and wiped his nose at the same time. When I opened the door to the chicken coop, my little brother scooted behind me for protection and we both set out to face Abe, the watch goat.

● ● ● ● ●

Dear Dad,

Since you couldn't be at Nanna's funeral, I thought I'd tell you about it—help to make you a memory since you're not here. I never knew that Nanna had so many friends. The church was packed with people, and they were all talking about her. It sure didn't seem like they were talking about the Nanna I knew. It's a good thing they could still remember Nanna before the Alzheimer's (Grandma taught me how to spell it) changed her so much. Lots of people loved Nanna like I do.

Another interesting thing happened. The night after the funeral, I had a dream. In this dream, Grandma was out in the garden pulling weeds like she always does, so I decided to go out and help. But when I made it to the edge of the garden, I heard someone singing, so I turned around to see who it was. And there was Nanna. She was sitting on the covered bench swing, rocking a little baby in her arms. She even looked up at me and smiled.

I'd never heard Nanna sing before, but her voice was beautiful. And so was the baby in her arms. I felt like I loved them both. Mom says that Nanna must be in Heaven watching over us and our little baby in Mom's tummy. I think she is.

One last thing, Dad. I hope you don't mind that I gave Spencer your black baseball cap. He seemed to need it more than me. I know I can be your big helper even if I'm not wearing the hat. All I have to do is think about you. After all, I've got a pretty great memory.

I love you, Dad. I miss you too!

Love, Allie—your Cracker Jack girl

12

Keeping Traditions

(Four months later)

The cool thing about living in Edna, Idaho, is that when it comes to picking out a Christmas tree, if you want to cut one down yourself, you don't have to go to a special Christmas tree farm. You just have to get a permit from the ranger, drive a half-hour up into the mountains, and pick out any old tree you want. It's as simple as that—well, except for the sawing part. And with Mom's belly sticking out halfway to China, and Dad still in Iraq, I almost began to wonder if maybe we should just pick out a tree from the Wal-Mart parking lot—almost!

But then, when I thought back on all the years that Mom, Dad, me, and Spencer went out and cut down our own tree, I knew that nothing in the world—not a war in Iraq, a pregnant Mom, or even a worried Grandma—could keep us from continuing our tradition.

And Grandma . . . she was worried—even a bit mad. As the three of us—Mom, me, and Spencer— hurried around the big yellow house, layering on our winter coats, hats, boots, mittens, and scarves, Grandma (who was in the kitchen heating up the hot cocoa) kept mumbling words and phrases to herself like "foolishness," "death-of-cold," "not my responsibility," and "always was a strong-willed child." But Mom didn't seem worried, so I figured I shouldn't be either.

When we finished loading the saw, some rope, a thermos of hot-cocoa, and a bag of Styrofoam cups into The Bruise, Mom asked Grandma one last time.

"So are you coming, Mother?"

Grandma started in again. "In your present

condition, why can't you make an exception this year?" Her voice sounded a bit like mine does when I'm asking if I can stay up an extra hour at night. "You're only two weeks from having this baby and in no position to be wandering around in the mountains, *in the snow*, chopping down trees."

"Tree, Mother . . . one tree," Mom was holding up her index finger.

"A Christmas tree." Spencer added.

"We do this every year, Grandma. We can't stop now. *We just can't!*" Now *I* was starting to sound like I do when I'm asking if I can stay up an extra hour at night.

When Grandma looked into my eyes, the expression on her face softened just a bit. "Oh . . . all right," she finally said. "But let's just go up the road into the foothills. I'm sure the pine trees there are just as wonderful as any other place."

Mom smiled as she put one arm around Grandma and pulled her into a squeeze—kind of like a half-hug. Mom did a lot of half-hugs and leaning hugs these days. It was all she could manage with that huge belly full of baby always getting in the way.

It wasn't much longer before the four of us— five if you count Mom's belly—headed out in The Bruise in search of the next Claybrook family Christmas tree. The excitement building inside of me seemed to be measured by the level of snow on the ground. When we left the big yellow house, the brown fields were covered in a thin layer of frost. But now as we drove up toward the hills, the frost had turned to a thick coat of snow. I couldn't wait to get out into it—to feel it, to taste it, to play in it, to make a whole new memory in it.

We never had to walk through snow to find our Christmas tree before. As a matter of fact, one year we didn't even need to wear coats and hats when we picked out our tree. Christmas tree hunting was a lot different in Idaho than it was in Texas. I bet spending Christmas in Iraq would be even more different.

"Will Dad have a Christmas tree this year?" I asked.

"I bet the Army has some nice trees set up somewhere for the soldiers to enjoy." Grandma was finally sounding cheerful again, but for some reason I couldn't seem to associate the idea of Dad spending Christmas in Iraq and sharing a tree that he didn't even cut down himself with a bunch of other soldiers as something to be cheerful about.

"I bet it'll be a fake tree." I mumbled, but no one seemed to hear. Mom had pulled The Bruise into a little turnout in the side of the road and all attention was now focused on our surroundings.

We were there—Christmas tree paradise! All

those people searching for a tree in the Wal-Mart parking lot had no idea what they were missing. The entire side of the hill was thick with snow-covered pine trees of every size.

After pulling my hat and gloves back on, I opened the car door and stepped out onto the perfect white snow. The surface was glistening in the sun like tiny, shimmering crystals. I liked the crunchy sound my boots made with each step. I liked the crispness of the air. I liked Christmas tree hunting in Idaho.

"Wait for me," Spencer hollered. I turned around to see my little brother trying his best to run toward me in a puffy green snowsuit. If it had been white, I might have confused him for a snowman or a marshmallow. I also noticed that over his blue beanie he was wearing Dad's baseball cap. I was really glad Spencer had remembered to bring it. Somehow, it made me feel better knowing that a little part of Dad was with us on this special day.

Spencer pointed to a pine tree that was probably as tall as a two-story house. "I want that one."

"And who's going to put the star all the way up on top of that huge thing?" Grandma asked.

"I will." Spencer volunteered. "I can climb like a monkey. Wanna see?"

"*NO!*" Mom and Grandma hollered at the

same time. Then Mom softened her voice. "The tree can't be taller than the ceiling in Grandma's living room."

We continued to walk through the snow, leaving footprints and making memories with each step.

"How about that one?" Spencer hollered. We all looked in the direction his finger was pointing until our eyes landed on a much shorter, perfectly shaped pine tree.

I hurried over to the tree, and when Mom reached it, she pulled Spencer in for one of those half-hugs. "I think you found it. What do you think, Allie?"

Before responding, I slowly wandered around the entire tree, examining every branch and pine needle. Choosing a Christmas tree was serious business, and since Dad wasn't here, and Mom being pregnant and all, I figured it was my responsibility to make sure we made the right choice.

I pulled down on one of the snow-covered branches and then let go. It swung back into place, sending a shower of snow crystals shimmering through the air. That familiar smell of pine sent a wave of memories of past Claybrook family Christmas trees throughout my entire body.

I was satisfied.

This was the perfect Christmas tree.

But we were only halfway finished. We still needed to saw it down.

"Me first, me first, me first." Spencer yelped like a little puppy dog—I swear, the kid must be half animal. He was trying to grab the saw out of Mom's hands, when Grandma put both of her hands on his shoulders to settle him down.

"You'll get your turn, young man. But you need to be very careful. A saw is *not* a toy."

Spencer turned away from Grandma so his body was facing me. He scrunched up his nose and mouth, and I had to hold my breath so I wouldn't laugh—not an easy thing, by the way, but somehow I managed. The kid could be pretty funny at times—irritating, but funny.

After posing in front of our tree to take a few pictures for Dad, it was time to get busy. Ignoring Grandma's complaints, Mom managed to get down onto her knees in the snow to help Spencer saw at the base of our perfect Christmas tree. After about forty-five seconds, the kid was begging to do it on his own. Mom finally let him but held out her arms only a few inches away from his gloved hands that were clutched to the saw's handle. Spencer's attempts at sawing down the tree lasted for maybe three whole seconds before he nearly bent the saw in half.

Since Mom was still on her knees, she gave it

another minute or two at the saw before finally giving up. Then she looked at me.

"Want to give it a try?"

"Yeah!"

At first it felt awkward trying to work the blade of the saw back and forth into the tree trunk. It kept getting stuck, and I almost wanted to give up. But then a thought occurred to me. Who would cut down our tree if I didn't? With her big belly poking out, Mom couldn't; Spencer couldn't either. Grandma didn't even want to be up here. She only came because she was worried about Mom's belly. She'd rather pick out a tree in the Wal-Mart parking lot, or worse yet, buy a fake one!

I guess it was up to me to actually keep our family tradition.

It took a while, but I finally got into an even rhythm—that seemed to help. It was hard work, though, and I really had to stay focused. After a while I could feel Mom's hand on my shoulder, and I could hear her voice asking me if I wanted to take a break. Except for giving a quick shake of my head, I was too busy to respond.

While the blade of the saw moved back and forth, my body began to heat up inside the layers of winter clothes. I almost wanted to stop and pull off my hat or take off my coat, but I didn't want to break my rhythm. Didn't want to break the tradition. Didn't want to lose another single thing in my life.

Back and forth, my arms pumped. My muscles began to burn. Back and forth my memory raced as the smell of pine and sawdust mixed in the air, filling my nose.

Dad, the "Tickle Monster," wearing his black baseball cap and chasing me and Spencer around our living room in Texas. A silly old goat named Abraham Lincoln thinks he's a watch dog. Penny Pickett picked a peck of pink pickled peppers . . . and her mom Trudy ate them all up . . . chewing with her mouth open. Mom's belly, growing, growing, growing . . . like the watermelons from Grandma's garden. Nanna wearing a sweater and sitting on the covered bench swing, watching Grandma work in the garden. Nanna watching me from heaven . . . remembering who I am . . . remembering that my name is Allie.

I was suddenly jarred out of my thoughts by a cracking sound. I quit sawing at the same moment that Mom put her hands on my aching shoulders, pulling me away from the falling tree.

"Timber!" Spencer yelled as the Claybrook family Christmas tree fell to the frozen ground. Grandma was clapping. Spencer was jumping up and down. Mom was giving me a half-hug. I was breathing—hard.

It took all four of us to lug the Christmas tree

back to The Bruise. I hadn't actually thought we walked that far to find a tree, but it seemed super far on the trek back to the car with ankle-deep snow slowing us down, and pine needles poking up my nose. Then it probably took another half an hour to get it on top of The Bruise and tie it down. When we'd finished, I was more than ready for some hot chocolate.

By the time we arrived back at the big yellow house and got the tree off the minivan, it was almost dark and I was tired. My entire body—especially my shoulders and arms—felt weak.

After gobbling down a peanut butter and jelly sandwich, I hiked up the green carpeted stairs in search of my warm bed. Not even the snores of my little brother or the creaking of a hundred-year-old house could keep me awake tonight. I was glad tomorrow was Sunday. I'd definitely be sleeping in.

I was surprised that my nose didn't wake up to the usual smells of Grandma's yummy breakfasts. Maybe she was so tired from yesterday that she decided to sleep in too. I kind of doubted that. Grandma *never* slept in.

When I walked down the stairs and into the kitchen I was surprised to see Spencer sitting at the table eating a bowl of cold cereal. And I was even more surprised to see Trudy Pickett sitting next to him. I was relieved she was only sipping from a glass of orange juice.

"Where's Mom . . . and Grandma?" I asked.

Spencer tried to say something, but I couldn't understand because his mouth was full of Coco Puffs.

I looked over at Trudy Pickett—not to accuse her of teaching my brother bad eating habits—he already had them without her help—but to figure out what was going on.

"She's at the hospital, sweetie." Trudy said. "Your Grandma took her last night, and I slept here."

My heart panicked—until I realized that Trudy was smiling and so was Spencer.

"The baby came out . . . he came out of Mom's tummy last night." Spencer finally spoke so I could understand.

"*He* . . . you mean a boy . . . another brother?"

Spencer just nodded his head and smiled.

So did I.

● ● ● ● ●

Dear Dad,

Guess what? Mom had our baby last night . . . or maybe it was this morning. Anyway, he is so cute! He even has dark hair like me. Mom says he has your mouth and nose. I'm not quite sure how she can tell something like this, but Grandma and Trudy Pickett agreed. Right now, I think his face is just kind of red and puffy.

Remember how I said I wanted a baby sister? Well, after I held our little baby today (Mom still doesn't know what to call him) I decided that maybe little brothers aren't that bad after all . . . especially when they're too young to make animal noises.

I love and miss you, Dad.

Love, Allie

P.S. We picked out a really cool Christmas tree and I practically cut it down all by myself. You would have been proud of me . . . like I'm proud of you.

Make Me a Memory Reader's Guide

Characters and Their Characteristics

In a book, the **characters** are the people who are in the story. A character could even be an animal. Most stories have a **main character**. Who is the main character in this story?

A **characteristic** is something unique about a person, such as hair or eye color or even something different about the way the person acts or does things. What is a unique characteristic about you?

Describe the following characters as you imagine them—how they look, how old you think they are, and what their personality is like. What are their unique characteristics?

Allie

Spencer

Mom

Dad

Grandma

Nanna

Abraham Lincoln (the goat)

Buster (the dog)

Discussion Questions

Why is Allie upset about leaving Killeen, Texas?

Have you ever had to move? How did it make you feel?

How does Allie feel about living in Edna, Idaho? Have you ever been to a small town like Edna, Idaho? Did you like it there? Would you like living in a small town?

Who are some of the people (and animals) Allie meets in Edna?

How does Allie feel about Abe, the goat? Why does their relationship change throughout the story?

How does Allie feel when she sees Nanna for the first time?

What disease does Nanna have? What does Allie call it, and why? Do you know anyone with Alzheimer's disease?

What are some of the things Nanna forgets?

What are some of the things Nanna remembers?

Why is Allie's Dad in Iraq?

Why is the black baseball hat so important to Allie? What does it represent (symbolize)?

Why do you think Allie gives Spencer Dad's black baseball cap near the end of the story?

Why does Allie feel it's so important to go and cut down a Christmas tree instead of buying one that was already cut?

Family Traditions

What is a family tradition?

Why are family traditions important?

List three traditions you have in your family.

List three traditions you would like to start with your family.

How far?

Have you ever wondered how far away your home is from other cities—even other countries? Allie often thought about just how far away she was from her dad while he was in Iraq. Edna, Idaho, is a fictitious town. But Killeen, Texas, is real. It's the home of Fort Hood Army Base. Do you have any idea how far away Killeen, Texas, is from, Baghdad, Iraq? If you guessed 7,364 miles, you are correct!

Activity:

Pick two locations and figure out how far away from each other they are. You can find your answer in an atlas or even online. (Helpful websites: www.mapquest.com or www.indo.com/distance).

Fun Facts about Goats!

If you loved Abraham Lincoln (the goat, not the president), then maybe you'll love these:

• 95 percent of the world's goats live in developing nations (countries with low average income compared to the world average).

• A female is called a doe, or nanny goat; a male is called a buck, or billy goat; and a baby is called a kid.

• When goats are pregnant, you say they are kidding.

• Goats are used to clear brush (by eating it), pull carts, produce fiber for clothing, and provide meat and milk.

- Worldwide, more people drink goat's milk than cow's milk. Many babies, children, and even adults who are unable to digest cow's milk, drink goat's milk instead.
- Did you know you can call a goat a butthead and be technically correct? Goats with horns are sometimes referred to as buttheads because they often butt heads. Ouch!
- Both male and female goats can have beards.
- Goats love to be brushed but hate it when people touch their ears.
- A goat has no teeth in the upper front of its mouth. But don't put your hand in its mouth because the teeth it does have are razor sharp.

For more goat information, check out these websites: http://www.uga.edu/~lam/kids/goats/doctor.html and http://www.abc.net.au/creaturefeatures/facts/goats.htm

Making Memories

Here are some suggestions on ways you can preserve the memories you have made:

- Keep a journal or diary and write in it regularly.
- Draw pictures of things, people, or places you want to remember. Be sure to put your name, the date, and your age somewhere on the front or back of your artwork.
- Make a Memory Book (a scrap book for all of your memories). Take pictures of an event or person. After the pictures are developed, place them in your Memory Book. Decorate the page, and don't forget to label the pictures.
- Video or tape record a conversation with a special person or an event.
- If there is a big event of local (or even national) interest that you want to remember, cut out clippings from the newspaper and place them in your Memory Book.
- Write regular letters (or e-mail) to someone and keep a copy for yourself. Put them in your Memory Book.

Short-Term Memory Games

Now You See It, Now You Don't

Present a tray full of ten or twenty small items to the class. Explain that students have only one minute to memorize the items on the tray. After one minute, cover the tray and have the students write down as many items as they can remember.

Something's Missing

This is a variation on the previous game. After the first game, remove one item from the tray and then present it to the children to see if anyone can remember what item is missing. (Before you start this game, collect the lists from the previous game).

Someone's Missing

Have one child step outside while a child inside the class is appointed to hide. Have the child outside come back in and see if he can figure out who is missing.

Scrambled Classroom

Have a few students leave the classroom. While they are gone, change the locations of several items in the class (be sure someone keeps track of the changes). Have the children re-enter the classroom and figure out which items are out of place and where they belong.

About the author

Tamra Norton attended Ricks College and Idaho State University, where she majored in English. She started her writing career with a column published in the *Fort Bend Sun*. Called "The Home Front," it depicted the antics of home life. Tamra's passion, however, is creating tales of fiction.

She enjoys reading in the bathtub, camping in the living room, and dancing in the kitchen. When she isn't gazing vacantly into the computer screen in the middle of the night, she is involved in home schooling her children and avoiding the guilt associated with lack of exercise and overindulgence in chocolate.

At the 2003 Society of Children's Book Writers and Illustrators conference in Houston, Tamra received the Joan Lowery Nixon Award for her middle-grade manuscript *Make Me a Memory*. She is also the author of *Molly Mormon?*, *Molly Married?*, *Molly Mommy?*, and *Comfortable in My Own Genes*.

Tamra lives in Spring, Texas, with her husband, Dennis. They are the parents of seven children. She welcomes comments and feedback from her readers. Feel free to visit her website at www.tamranorton. com, or send her an e-mail at tamra@tamranorton.com.

0 26575 78669 9